THE JAWS OF DEATH!

Milo had never seen anything like this beast before. It was as big as a black bear and its jaws were filled with biting, tearing teeth.

This one will come in low to the ground and very fast, he thought. And he had just set himself to stab t the head of the beast when the toothy head and the rest of the creature lunged at him with what seemed the speed of light. His too-high spear blade just slid across the top of the beast's flat head, slashing only the edge of a black ear.

And as he raised his spear again to ward the creature off, Milo felt the sudden burning agony of sharp teeth tearing through the thick leather of his boot and into the flesh of his leg beneath. . . .

HORSECLANS #15

ROBERT ADAMS

THE MEMORIES OF MILO MORAI

A SIGNET BOOK

NEW AMERICAN LIBRARY

NAL BOOKS ARE AVAILABLE AT QUANTITY DISCOUNTS WHEN USED TO
PROMOTE PRODUCTS OR SERVICES. FOR INFORMATION PLEASE WRITE TO
PREMIUM MARKETING DIVISION, NEW AMERICAN LIBRARY, 1633 BROADWAY,
NEW YORK, NEW YORK 10019.

SIGNET TRADEMARK REG. U.S.PAT. OFF AND FOREIGN COUNTRIES
REGISTERED TRADEMARK—MARCA REGISTRADA
HECHO EN CHICAGO, U.S.A.

SIGNET, SIGNET CLASSIC, MENTOR, ONYX, PLUME, MERIDIAN and NAL
BOOKS are published by New American Library
1633 Broadway, New York, New York 10019

First Printing, August, 1986

1 2 3 4 5 6 7 8 9

PRINTED IN THE UNITED STATES OF AMERICA

For Richard Curtis,
For John Silbersack,
and for
Michael Aaron Johnson,
born 2 October 1985.
The three new men in my life.

Prologue

Still and unmoving as two statues, the men sat,
waiting for one of the browsing, slowly shifting herbivores to wander within range of the short, powerful
bows with which they were armed. The spring was
now far enough advanced for the beasts to have begun
to fatten, and so, even after they had been dressed out,
two of them should provide food for all of the party for
which the men were hunting this day. Slouched
forward over the necks of their grazing horses, in
constant telepathic contact with their mounts and
with each other, the two ignored the flies that crawled
upon them, the sweat that poured from them under
the hot sun and the reek of the fresh deer dung with
which they had liberally smeared their hands and
faces to cover the smell of predatory man from their
prey.

The herd they stalked was mixed—shaggy, feral
cattle, shaggier bison, an assortment of deer and an
even wider-ranging assortment of antelope, a few
gazelles, a few wild horses and burros, even the
occasional wild goat or two. The progenitors of the
animals making up the herd had been natives of
widely separated habitats on four continents, and a
few hundred years before that spring day on the

prairie of North America, no one of the billions of humans then living would ever have seen a like herd on any of those four. But those billions of humans died long ago, precious few of them living long enough to breed and leave descendants, and the species of mankind now was the rarest of creatures upon the grassy lands, moving only in small, scattered bands with his domestic herds among the tumbled, overgrown ruins of his brief hegemony, gathering and hunting for the bulk of his food, taking only milk and blood and fiber from his precious herds save in the direst of emergencies.

Heads well down, giving every appearance of doing nothing more than grazing the fetlock-high grasses, the brace of telepathically controlled hunting horses slowly moved closer to the mixed herd, drawing little if any attention from the wary, chary prey of the motionless hunters, who had steeled themselves to not even wince at the bites of the flies, for the meat that they sought here was of importance to those back in camp.

But although they made no slightest sound, still they conversed. "Gy," beamed the elder to the younger, "what is the nearest animal to me? Can you see?"

"Yes, Uncle Milo," beamed back the younger, who was a bit more slender than the elder, though seemingly as tall and strong-looking, with rolling muscles. "A white, brown-faced ridged-horn . . . a big one, a buck. A few more yards and you'll be at the right range. And me?"

The elder blinked the sweat away to clear his vision slightly and silently replied, "A yellow deer and two spotted ones, close together. The yellow one looks to be best; he's young and seems a little fatter than the other two. No antlers, of course, but I'd bet that he's a spike buck. You are within range of him already."

At his rider's unspoken urging, the stallion bearing the elder of the two men moved farther forward, closer to the fringes of the widely scattered aggregation of grazers and browsers. Obligingly, the antelope that was his quarry finished stripping the leaves and shoots from a tall weed and chose that moment to move toward another plant, this one even closer to the hunger.

"*Now*, Uncle Milo, *now!*" came the imperative message from the younger man's mind to the elder's.

Within the bare space of a breath, the two men straightened, brought up the bows with the already-nocked arrows, drew, aimed and sent the shafts thudding into the two beasts. The shaft of the younger man sank into the eye of the deer and penetrated the brain, and the stricken beast dropped without so much as a sound or a movement. The loosing of the elder man went in behind the near shoulder of the whitish antelope and skewered lung and heart, yet the mortally wounded animal would have fled had not the man brought his horse close enough to lean from his saddle and take firm grip of one of the pair of sharp-tipped horns, lift the heavy beast almost clear of the ground and hold it against its struggles until it went limp.

Within the herd, pandemonium raged unchecked. Joining forces as they often did in the face of danger, the feral cattle and the bison drew into a tight formation, their vulnerable calves in the center, the wicked horns of the bulls and cows on the perimeter. But all around this defensive grouping, the smaller beasts fled madly in every direction, some of them in aggregations of their species, some as individuals.

Watching a band of graceful impala leap impossibly high in their flight to land and immediately leap again took the elder man's mind racing backward over the intervening centuries to his days of soldiering in Africa. So, too, did the rapid departure of a group of fast if ungainly-looking wildebeests.

"All that's missing," he thought, "are the zebras and the lions."

Not that both of those had not adapted over the years to life on portions of the vast, endless-seeming prairies and plains of the North American continent, but there were none of the stripped equines running with this particular portion of the great herds, and the lion prides did not hunt every day.

The two men, younger and elder, cooperated in roughly, hurriedly field-dressing the two slain beasts, then took the carcasses up in front of them on the withers of their mounts and set off for camp before the smell of fresh-spilled blood drew to the spot predators and scavengers too big or too numerous for them to handle. As they rode away with their booty, they left behind a section of prairie now host only to the close-packed formation of bison and long-horned cattle, all of the other beasts of the former mixed herd now having become but dots, some still moving, in the far distance.

Nearly two hours of easy-paced riding brought them within sight of their camp—four round felt yurts and as many high-wheeled carts, some threescore horses wandering, grazing around the edges of the campsite, standing belly-deep in the shallow lakelet near which the camp had been made or sipping water from the chuckling stream that issued from it.

As they approached the lakeside camp, the elder of the hunters—a man called Milo Morai or Uncle Milo —tried to picture in his mind's eye a memory of the map of this country as it had been so many long years in the past. He thought that they were probably in northern Oklahoma now, possibly southern Kansas, surely not far enough west to be in Texas still. They had wintered in Texas, camping with Kindred Clans Staiklee and Gahdfree, and now they were headed northeastward.

Milo meant to strike farther east than usual in hopes of finding ruins from the world before this one that had not been so thoroughly picked over and picked through as had those along the central migration routes of the game herds and the Kindred clans. Usable metals and singular artifacts gleaned from such ruins were not only valuable in their own right, useful to the nomads of the clans, but they also could be bartered for other useful things with the wagon-borne eastern traders who ventured out upon the prairies each spring and summer from the more populous areas beyond the great waterway of the Mississippi River.

As the well-laden horses ambled nearer to the camp, a very pretty, very pregnant blond girl kneeling before one of the yurts looked up from her chore of grinding grain and awkwardly rose to her feet, shouting, "Myrah, Gy and Uncle Milo are back with two kills."

A mindspeak answered her, beaming, "Aha! Two men, two kills, that should clyster some of the overweening pride out of that gaggle of silly Staiklee and Gahdfree boys, I should think. They were out all morning with their yapping spotted dogs and draggled in with nothing more than a half-dozen scrawny rabbits."

"But they did find a ruin, Myrah, quite a large one, too. And you know how anxious Uncle Milo and Bard Herbuht have been to get to a ruin that has not been looted before. That should count for at least something," the pregnant blonde beamed back. "The Staiklee and Gahdfree boys mean well, you know. You are too hard on them—you fault them too much for their high spirits and their tale-spinnings."

"Meaning well never yet filled a stewpot," was the silent reply. "Nor did bragging, out-and-out lying and the taking of stupid chances of the like of juggling sharp knives while standing on one's head in the saddle of a galloping horse; little children sometimes do things like those, Karee, but remember these are supposed to be young, proven warriors, all blooded and ready to take their places in the warrior-councils of their clans after they have ridden out as guards with the traders for a season or two. My father, the Skaht of Skaht, would have—"

Karee Skaht Linsee had had enough, however. "Your father, Myrah, owns all of my respect as the good chief he has been, but every one of us clansfolk knows and has long known that where it concerned you, he had a large soft spot in his head. You are and have always been a spoiled brat. You're dead certain that only your desires, only your beliefs, should have any value. You had better thank Sacred Sun that our Gy is a basically gentle man, for you've richly deserved a sound thrashing for months . . . and he still may tan your hide, if your intemperate beamings and outbursts continue to embarrass him and Uncle Milo and Bard Herbuht.

"Now, get your lazy, slugabed self out here and do some real work, for a change!"

But only Karee, Bard Herbuht's two wives—the middle-aged Mai and the slightly younger Djinee— and his nine-winters-old daughter, Kai, were on hand when the two hunters led their horses into the flat area on which the yurts fronted. Gy frowned and sent a private beam, and presently his other wife, Myrah, stepped sullenly out of the yurt.

As she helped the elder hunter to untie the stiff carcass of the whitish antelope, Karee remarked, "Uncle Milo, the young warriors have found a ruined place, a large one, they say. And although they all say they have hunted in this area before, they also say that none of them had ever come across this place or even suspected that one lay hereabouts. They didn't get much game, though, only a few rabbits. And another of their spotted dogs disappeared last night, too."

"Good." He nodded. "Thank you for telling me of it, Karee. But where are my wives, Djoolya and Verah?"

She waved an arm to indicate general direction. "Away over on the other side of the little lake, I think. They went out shortly after you and Gy rode off. They are looking for roots and greens. Two of the Staiklee warriors are with them, looking for any traces of the missing dogs."

"What of the other Staiklees and the two Gahdfree boys, Karee?" inquired Milo.

She shrugged. "Downstream somewhere, with hopes of arrowing or spearing or catching fish or frogs, they said." Then she wrinkled up her brows and said, "This is another of those peculiar deerlike things, Uncle Milo—what did you say the folk of ancient days called them? I'd never before seen any of this kind until we came into this country."

"They were called addaks, Karee. And, no, they never seem to be found here anywhere north of southern Kansas, and they're none too common even here, but they're good eating and their hides make good leather. With this one and the big young buck that Gy dropped, all of the camp will eat well this night, at least, even the cats. Where are the cats, anyway?"

"Out guarding the horses, I suppose, Uncle Milo. None of them has come into camp today, all day long, although I've seen Snowbelly and Spotted One both drinking from the lake at various times, since the nooning."

After a nod of thanks to the young woman, Milo sent a mindcall ranging out and was immediately rewarded by the answering beamings of all three of the cats. "The twoleg Gy and I both killed fourleg grasseaters," he informed the felines. "So there will be offal for you all, shortly, as well as some odds and ends of rabbit and maybe fish and frogs."

Pleased and pleasantly anticipatory beamings came from the two prairiecats, but the "tame" jaguar, Spotted One, replied, "This cat killed and fed last night, twoleg cat friend Milo, so let the other two cats come in to eat—Spotted One will keep watch over the herd."

Milo had had his doubts about just how well the wild-born and -bred jaguar was going to work out living with the Horseclans, for all that she had voluntarily joined with the prairiecat Crooktail in fighting off a pack of hyenas that had killed a mare, a foal and a boy farther north in the previous year, but the wild feline had laid his fears to rest; she had never once made to attack any horse, bovine, sheep or goat or their young. She usually kept a sizable physical distance from twolegs, which was understandable enough, though she was civil and very cooperative when mindspoken and, more important, she was carrying a litter sired by Snowbelly, which last meant to Milo that the singular race of prairiecats—the result of a succession of breeding experiments ended by the nuclear and biological warfare that had all but extirpated mankind worldwide—was more *Leo* than *Felis*. Now if the kittens she bore proved to be fertile, rather than mere sterile hybrids, there never again would be any need to subject the race to possibly deleterious inbreeding.

The skinning had been accomplished, the cleaning and butchering were underway, and the two prairiecats were crouched feeding on the tender, bloody offal before the four Kindred warriors rode up from the southwest, whooping exuberantly, bearing strings of assorted fish and a brace of sizable writhing, decapitated vipers.

A short time later, five horses, four of them with riders, were seen to crest the low rise of ground on the opposite side of the lake and head around the water toward the campsite. The led packhorse bore two bulging sacks and a huge caldron, discolored with thick verdigris and with bits of loam still adhering to it. As the party drew closer, it could be seen that, though clothed similarly, two were adult women and two, young warriors.

Arriving in the central space, the elder of the two women—an auburn-haired, green-eyed, stocky woman of between thirty-five and forty winters—slid easily from her saddle, strode back to the packhorse and began to loose the big caldron from its load, mind-speaking the while.

"Milo, love, this lovely pot came from a place about three miles northeast of here. It's either copper or brass and so *big*, you could feed a whole clan out of it. And the pot's not all, either—wait until you see what else Verah and I found."

The next morning, while Bard Herbuht rode out for his day of hunting with Little Djahn Staiklee and Djim-Djoh Staiklee, Milo took Gy Linsee, the four remaining Teksikuhn Kindred warriors and a cart and they all followed his premier wife, Djoolya, to the place where she had found the large copper caldron. In addition to their normal, everyday weapons, they bore along spades, axes, a wooden maul and assortment of wedges, a wagon jack and some hardwood pry-poles, strong ropes and a hand-carved wooden pulley.

First sight of the place from the crest of a low hill was most disheartening, however. Although patterns of vegetative growth gave indications of where the edges of fields and pastures had been so long ago, nothing resembling a building remained. Up close, the clearing away of vines and brush and bushes revealed fire-blackened stones and crumbly concrete. Between the walls of what had once been a large, rambling structure, beneath several centuries' worth of soil and decomposing vegetation, was a jumbled layer of cracked and shattered sheets of slate, and below that layer, ancient charcoal that had once been thick beams and joists.

Early on, they disturbed two rattlesnakes, but quick slashes of sabers took off the reptiles' heads, and, tied together by the tails over a tree limb, the bodies were left to thrash and drain and later become part of the daily meal of the camp.

Bits and pieces of rusted iron and steel and corroded, discolored other metals were scattered all through the charcoal layer—nails, screws, hinges, doorknobs and locks, wire lengths, piping lengths, little solidified pools of copper and brass and lead. In one room they unearthed a sizable chunk of solid silver protruding out of which were several rusting, pointless knifeblades. This find and the other melted nonferrous metals went into the cart, along with the copper and brass and any hardware items not too rusty or deformed to be of further use. Another find that brought a smile to Milo's face was a complete, relatively undamaged set of hearth tools of heavy, solid bronze. More treasures were dug out of a room close to the one wherein the chunk of melted silver had been found—more than a dozen pans and pots of copper with brass handles, some plates and utensils of brass and of pewter, including a magnificent pewter mug that looked to Milo as if it would hold at least two quarts of liquid. That these finds had not melted of the heat of the long-ago fire verged on the miraculous. Most of the steel cutlery had become only lengths of flaking rust, but a few blades still were found sound, along with a sharpening steel and a dozen tinned skewers, a large, two-tined fork and a copper ladle.

Apparently, not one item of glass or china or earthenware in that room had remained whole, and shards of them littered the subsurfaces. Such pieces of plastics and aluminum as turned up were brittle and useless.

A hump in the center of this space proved, upon clearance, to be a large, rust-flaking double-door refrigerator-freezer unit.

"We'll take this apart," said Milo, adding, "The amounts of copper tubing and wiring will make it worth the effort."

It was when Milo, Gy and the two Staiklees raised the thing up from its centuries-old grave that they found what lay beneath it.

When Milo and the muscular Gy, between them, were able to get the trapdoor open, foul, musty air poured up from the utter darkness below. Turning to the Staiklees, he said, "We're going to need some torches down there."

And so they did, but only until Milo found and filled up and lit some gasoline lanterns that were in the cellar. He reflected that this cache would have been a true treasure trove two or three hundred years ago, but not now. True, there still was more than enough of value to him and to his people contained unspoiled in the sometime fallout shelter, but there was much else that now was utterly useless if not downright dangerous.

He had the seven bodies—two men, two women and three children—dragged into the room that had been the pantry, no pleasant task, as they had all begun to decompose as soon as the fresh, moist outer air got to them. That done, they began to load whatever looked usable or tradable onto the cart, and when it would hold no more, they sent Little Djahn Staiklee to drive it back to the campsite and bring back an empty one.

While searching for an easier way and possibly a wider opening to get their gleanings up to the surface, Milo found a short flight of steps leading up to an angled pair of doors, but they refused to budge a millimeter, even to the efforts of all three of the men, plus those of Djoolya.

Outside, the reason why was clear. Also clear was just why no one of them had seen the doors before: they were completely covered by a portion of the fieldstone half-wall. When once the stones had been lifted and thrown off, the heavy, steel-sheathed doors opened with only a few minutes of straining and cursing and use of two of the pry-poles.

As they all squatted, panting, among the scattered stones, Milo beamed, "When first I saw them, I didn't think those folks in the pantry there died of the plagues—none of them bore any of the easily recognizable signs of that kind of dying. No, I think they all got trapped down there and smothered to death. Of course, it was really the fire that did them in; with half a ton of stone blocking one exit and that humongous refrigerator on the other, no two men and two women could possibly have used either opening. Their air intakes must have gotten blocked then or soon after, and that was all she wrote for the lot of them. That's why they didn't start to rot until we went down there, too—there was no oxygen in the place, no breathable air.

"Let's get them up here, out yonder somewhere, before they get any higher. The coyotes and foxes and buzzards will clean them up quickly if they can get at them.

"Since they didn't die of the plagues, that means we can take all the bedding, too, and those are nice, thick, warm-looking blankets. Whenever Little Djahn gets

back with an empty cart, we'll load it with the best of
the things down there, then close up the place to keep
animals out and come back tomorrow or the next day
to finish stripping it. Whatever any of you do, though,
leave the sealed metal containers and the glass jars and
bottles alone until I've had the chance to check out
their contents; old as they are, anyone who even tasted
of them would likely be poisoning himself."

"But Milo," demanded Djoolya, "what of all those
pretty jars? The traders exchange valuable things for
even one of those jars that has not been broken or
chipped at an edge and that still has its top. Surely we
aren't going to just leave them all here?"

He leaned toward her to pat her grubby, work-
roughened hand. "Oh, no, honey, we won't leave
them here. No, tomorrow or the next day, we'll come
back, dump whatever is in them out, pack them in a
cartload of dried grass as far as the lake, wash them
out well and put them somewhere safe to drain and
dry until we're ready to move on. I really hate to
dump out that much food, but it's all just too old to
take the chance that it might still be even edible. Lest
some Kindred clan wander through here and find and
foolishly or innocently try to open and eat of those
ancient cans, before we leave, we'll hump them all up
here and axe them open—a few poisoned coyotes
won't be any great loss."

Spitting out the grass stem he had been absently
chewing, Djim-Bahb Gahdfree asked, "What of those
two big handsome steel chests, Uncle Milo? We should
at least open them, I think, even if they prove too
heavy to take away from here."

Milo nodded. "They're not so heavy as they seem,
Djim-Bahb. I believe they're just bolted to the wall or
the floor or both. We will indeed open them, though
I'm pretty sure I know at least part of what we'll find
in them, and whenever two or three of you get back

from your clan camp with another cart for us, we'll load up those two steel chests and take them along with us. The traders should be overjoyed to get such artifacts still in such splendid condition, with built-in lockworks and the keys to fit them."

Gy Linsee raised an eyebrow quizzically. "*Keys*, Uncle Milo?"

Milo nodded. "You recall those rings of flat metal things I took off the belts of those two men's bodies, Gy? Those were called keys, and I'm sure that at least two of them will open those metal chests."

Before he and Gy left camp to hunt the next morning, Milo sent off Little Djahn and Djim-Bahb with spare mounts and a packhorse to seek out their clans' camp and dicker for the purchase of the spare cart, now needed. He had them take back the now-reduced gaggle of spotted dogs, as well, for despite all precautions, one dog per night was regularly disappearing from the campsite, and protracted searches for any trace of them had been completely unavailing.

Less than an hour out of camp, Milo and Gy were lucky enough to find a young screwhorn bull—an earlier age would have called him an eland—grazing alone, a mile or more from the herd of herbivores. It was in an area of rough, broken ground over which Milo would have been hesitant to pursue the beast on horseback, but the bull elected to stand and fight and so was quickly killed with arrows from a safe distance. Then, while Milo guarded the fresh kill, Gy went back at the gallop to fetch a cart and more hands to help with the job of skinning, cleaning, butchering and transporting nearly a half-ton of meat, bone and hide. So fortunate a kill would keep the camp well supplied for several days.

Nor was food alone the value of the bull. The hide would be rendered into fine, strong leather and the hair into felt. Horn would become tools and implements; sinew, thread for sewing or making ropes. When steel needles were not available, slivers of bone could be made to serve that purpose, and still other pieces of bone, after fire-hardening and sharpening, were often used to tip hunting arrows. Cleaned and soaked and carefully stretched, then dried, the bull's stomach pouches would become the inner linings of water containers; so too would his bladder. Hooves might be and often were rendered with fish offal to produce glue for a plethora of purposes, or sections cut from hooves made fine scaleshirts when sewed onto leather backing for war armor.

With the women, the children and Bard Herbuht fully occupied in camp, Milo took the cart down to the lake and washed off the blood, then he, Gy and two more of the Kindred warriors rode back to the ruin with the cart.

It was not yet noon when they arrived at their destination, but even so, the seven bodies dragged out and left upon the prairie on the afternoon before were already become only a few disjointed, widely scattered bones, all but invisible in the high grass.

As he had expected, the steel cabinets opened readily to two of the keys, and the contents were also about what he had been expecting, but more so.

The M-16s were there, three of them, but they were the selective-fire model, capable of full-automatic operation, which was unusual. There were four shotguns—two short pumps and two doubles—an M-3A1 submachine gun, two scoped hunting rifles, three .22 caliber rifles and a dozen handguns of assorted calibers and sizes. There was enough ammunition to start a small-scale war and four hand-grenades. But one of the steel ammunition boxes proved to contain not cartridges or explosives but coins—rolls of silver dimes, quarters, halfs, dollars and Mexican five- and ten-peso pieces, plus a few other rolls of gold Krugerrands, Mexican twenty- and fifty-peso pieces, and a few American gold pieces. This last box he took out and set aside.

All save one of the firearms he transferred to the larger of the steel cabinets, which was, he was glad to see, literally built into a corner of the room. After dropping the keys inside with the arms, munitions and grenades, he slammed the self-locking door upon the dangerous artifacts. There was no point in allowing any of the Horseclansmen to learn to use and depend upon weapons that they would find worse than useless after they had fired off all of the limited stocks of ammunition; bows and slings and darts had been sufficient to keep them fed and protected for nearly three hundred years now, and he had no intention of spoiling them with the incipiently deadly fruits of a long-dead technology.

The one pistol he retained was, he admitted to himself, partially a nostalgia trip. The .45 caliber M1A1 Government automatic was made mostly of stainless steel with a matte finish, but the heft and the feel were achingly familiar. He packed all of the .45 ammo he could turn up—five hundred plus rounds—the five magazines, the spare-parts kit, two holsters and a lanyard in a hinged, lockable 20mm ammo box, adding the .22 caliber conversion kit and a block of the small-caliber ammo for it, as well. The pistol would serve him as an emergency, last-ditch defensive weapon in its larger configuration and to take small game when traveling alone in its smaller. The time was quickly coming when he would be very glad that he had not locked away this weapon too.

Little Djahn Staiklee and Djim-Bahb Gahdfree came back into the camp in a little over a week— very good time for such a trip—both they and the two new young warriors who accompanied them back all whooping and chortling over their expertise at haggling. They had managed to convert the packhorse load of goods into not one but two carts, each of them complete with teams and harness, water barrels and spare parts and even kegs of grease for the axles and hubs, plus a twenty-pound sack of dried pinto beans and a fifty-pound sack of dry, shelled corn, both raided or traded from the Dirtmen by one or the other of the Kindred clans.

There were no spotted dogs with them when they returned, but in place of them were two big, wiry, tough-looking hounds of the sort that these southerly dog-clan folk called tooth-hounds—dogs bred and trained to hold dangerous game at bay and, if necessary, to close with and kill the beasts. Milo would have been happier if the young men had brought back no canines at all, but if they had to have dogs along, he agreed that these were the kind to have; any predator that chose to tangle with one or both of them would have its work cut out for it, no two ways about that matter.

During the afternoon and evening of the day of the return of Little Djahn Staiklee, everything but bare essentials was packed into the carts, and the next morning, the yurts were struck, folded and packed, the king stallion was requested to move the herd out and the party commenced a march to the environs of the large ruin that the young warriors had chanced across weeks before.

They moved like a migrating clan—Crooktail and Snowbelly ranging well out in front, zigzagging back and forth across the projected line of march, seeking out danger or game; next came the mounted warriors, riding well separated in a crescent that guarded both the van and the forward flanks; then came the six carts driven by the wives of Milo, Bard Herbuht and Gy Linsee; the horse herd followed, shepherded, kept moving, by the king stallion, Spotted One and Bard

Herbuht's children. At Milo's order, the brace of
tooth-hounds were led along on ropes tied to the tails
of two of the carts, for the prairiecats did not like
canines of any type or description and were big
enough, strong enough and fast enough to quickly
make a blood pudding of either of the dogs, if so
inclined. Only the jaguar, Spotted One, seemed at all
tolerant of the presence of the hounds on the march or
in camp.

The ready bows and throwing-sticks and slings of
the skirmish line of warriors garnered a goodly supply
of rabbits and three small antelope of as many kinds
during the day's march, and Little Djahn Staiklee
roped and strangled to death a large antelope, while
the redoubtable Snowbelly came back as far as the line
of horsemen dragging a large, fat, spotted sambar
buck.

Although they moved like a clan, the small party
moved much faster than a clan, lacking the slow,
difficult job of herding the cattle, sheep and goats kept
by clans for milk products and fiber. Therefore, they
had covered more than half the distance to their
objective by midafternoon and when they came upon
an ideal campsite, Milo ordered a halt.

Although no one, not even the prairiecats, suspected
it, however, they had been under observation
throughout the day, and they still were as they settled
into the night's camp.

Chapter 1

While the cats came into camp to eat, the young warriors and their two big dogs guarded the horse herd, not returning until the three feline guardians had once more assumed their vigil. When the party rode back in, Little Djahn Staiklee, the acknowledged leader of the group, sought out Milo.

"Uncle Milo, the horses all are restless this afternoon. The king stallion says that a strange cat has been sniffing around for days now, and it seems as if it trailed us here from the old campsite, too. You know, I'd been suspicioning that maybe Spotted One had been responsible for taking our hounds off, one at the time; teegrais always has had them a pure liking for dogmeat. But maybe I was wrong, Uncle Milo, maybe it's another teegrai, a wild one, been stalking around camp wherever we was."

Milo frowned. "Surely the cats would have noticed if any of their wild cousins were getting close enough to us to present any danger to the horses—though, knowing them and their inborn and unconcealed prejudices, they might have just neglected to mention any wild cat that was concentrating on killing, carrying off and eating dogs."

Staiklee nodded. "Well, the cat that tackles either of

the two tooth-hounds I brought back, Bearbane or Brutus, is going to purely have a bellyful of trouble before it gets a bellyful of anything else. Them two has killed or been in at the killing of bears, pigs, teegrais, tree-cats, wild bulls, bufflers and more kind of deers than you could shake a stick at. I raised and trained both of them out of a litter one my paw's bitches throwed by his lead tooth-hound, Ballbiter. They is two tough hounds, Uncle Milo. You never seen the like of them in all your born days."

"Probably not," replied Milo, adding, "Nonetheless, please keep both of those dogs in your yurt tonight; we all have another long, hard trek tomorrow, remember, and the very last thing that any of us—man or beast—needs this night is sleep-robbing excitement. Once we arrive at the new camp, then we'll see about this strange cat."

The night passed peacefully enough, but at daybreak, while the twolegs were nibbling their hard cheese and drinking down the mugs of a bastard brew that the far-southern Kindred clans called by the name of "kawfee," the two tooth-hounds, roaming out beyond the perimeter, began to make anxious-sounding noises.

At once, the young warriors dropped their mugs, crammed the last remnants of cheese into their mouths and lunged for weapons of the hunt—bows and quivers, darts, spears, slings, riatas and bolas. Even as they all trotted off in the direction from which came the canine sounds, Little Djahn Staiklee beamed to Milo, Bard Herbuht and Gy Linsee, "Brutus and Bearbane, they done found where something big and mean has been, sure as rain. They don't use that there tone for just deers or bulls or pigs and the like."

Fretfully, the middle-aged tribal bard beamed back, "If you lot want to go rambling off into that high grass down there after who knows what, then go; but you'd better leave at least a couple of you here to strike and load your yurt and gear, saddle your horses and hitch up your team. Otherwise, we'll leave them here. You must learn to honor precommitments under any circumstances."

"Djeri-Djai, Sami-Hal, you two stay back yonder and do for the rest of us, heanh?" Clearly grudgingly, the two young men trudged back up the hillock, stacked their weapons and commenced to strip the coverings from the frame of their yurt, muttering under their breaths to each other about elderly spoilsports.

While their women dismantled the yurts, Milo and Gy called in their mounts for this first part of the day's march and saddled them before calling in the cart horses and harnessing them. They had not quite, either of them, finished this last when a furious din erupted down on the prairie some hundreds of yards distant from the hilltop camp.

Their ears buffeted by snarls, barkings, growlings, human shouts and at least one agonized scream, Milo, Gy and Bard Herbuht ran to their saddled and equipped mounts and were quickly astride and all stringing bows. Mindcalling the two young warriors who were themselves about to mount, he said, "Not so fast. Call in the mounts of those out there and saddle them all before you leave here. If we three can't be of help in whatever is going on, then the addition of two more would be of no value either. And if this develops into a chase, everyone will be needing a horse, not just five of us."

As he passed out of camp at a fast walk, Djoolya ran over and placed in Milo's hand a six-foot hunting spear. The grass below the cleared hilltop was as high as or higher than a mounted man and grew more thickly with every yard they descended, severely hampering visibility if not movement, the rough, sharp edges of the grasses slashing at exposed hands and faces like so many knives.

But they did not need to see to find the scene of the bayed beast; they had ears, still, and the sounds of battle still smote them, not seeming to move fast or far. Bard Herbuht and Gy Linsee both nocked a shaft, grasping a brace of others between the fingers of their bow hands, ready for rapid loosings if need be. As they got nearer to the uproar, Milo beamed a mindcall to Little Djahn.

"What have the dogs cornered?"

"I don't know, Uncle Milo," came back the telepathic message, "and I thought I knowed every critter on the prairies and plains, too."

"Well, what does it look like?" beamed Milo. "No, don't try to tell me—open your mind and let me enter and see for myself, boy."

Milo had never seen anything exactly like the beast either. He thought it bore a vague resemblance to both the badger and the wolverine, though it looked more like a monstrous stoat or weasel. It was as big as a black bear, though far more slender, and most of its supple body was the color of dead grass, though its feet, legs and part of its tail were either black or very dark brown, as too were its ears and its muzzle. The jaws were filled with white teeth of a respectable size, most of those easily visible being cuspids—biting, tearing teeth. If there were more than just the one of these predators around . . . !

He mindcalled the king stallion, his warhorse, "Brother, take the herd onto the hilltop, where it's easier to see for a distance. Crooktail will stay with you, but I have need of the other cats."

Then he mindcalled Snowbelly, saying, "Cat brother, bring the Spotted One and come to the sounds here in the grass. There is a very singular beast here and I need to know if there is more than just this one about."

To Djoolya, he beamed, "Leave off whatever you're doing, you and all the others. String your bows and be ready for the herd to shortly come up there. Keep your eyes peeled for a light-tan-colored animal. It looks like a bear-sized weasel with black feet and tail and ears. Tell those boys that I said to stay up there, too. That herd is of more importance than anything else, and this thing is easily big enough to kill a horse or just about anything else that takes its fancy."

As the three riders finally cleared the patch of tall grasses, they could see the knot of men and beasts less than a hundred yards distant in a trampled-down area of two-foot grasses. The beast now bore a resemblance to a porcupine, so many were the arrow and dart shafts standing up from its snaky body, but apparently no one of those missiles had struck a really vital organ, for the beast still moved fast as greased lightning, as it tried its best to get a few teeth into the dancing, bleeding dogs and the cautiously stalking men. That it had already succeeded in its purpose more than once was evident from the gashed hounds and one of the young warriors who sat hunched over in the grass. Since the remaining five men were advancing with spears and bolas, Milo assumed that they had expended their supplies of arrows and darts.

To Gy, he beamed, "You're our best archer. If I can get the beast on my spear and hold him more or less still for an instant, do you think you could sink a shaft into one of his eyes?"

"All I can do is my best, Uncle Milo," was the reply.

Cursing himself for not having chosen to ride a trained and experienced hunting horse this day, Milo rode as close as he was able without losing all control of the nervous, clearly frightened dun gelding, then he slung his bowcase-quiver across his back, took his spear into his left hand long enough to wipe the sweaty palm of his right on his thigh, dismounted and trotted toward the fray.

Close up, the stink of musk almost took his breath away for a moment. Yes, this creature was definitely of the mustelid clan; whatever else it might be, that much was patent truth. He also now recalled where he had seen a creature—also a mustelid—that had at least a superficial resemblance to this one. The American plains ferret was colored almost exactly like this beast, but there the resemblance ended abruptly, for the few black-footed ferrets he had ever seen were none of them more than eighteen inches long, including the tail, where this one was, overall, a good eight feet or more.

"Call off the dogs," he beamed to Little Djahn Staiklee. "And try not to get into Gy Linsee's way. I'm going in and try to hold it on the spear long enough for Gy to put an arrow into its brain through an eye."

"Not alone you're not, Uncle Milo," Staiklee beamed back. "You don't know just how fast and supple that thing can be, and I do. No, I'll take Djim-Bahb's wolf spear and go in with you; that critter might dodge one point, but not two, and with any kind of luck, we'll get both of them into it."

Milo shrugged, then beamed to Gy, "This stubborn young Kinsman insists on going spearing with me, and I long ago learned the utter hopelessness of trying to get logic into the head of any of the Teksikuhn Kindred. Do you think you can do it with two of us there instead of just me?"

"As I said before, Uncle Milo," came the reply, "I can do but my best."

Milo tested the point and the whetted edges of the spearhead with a thumb, made certain that the steel crossbar below the head was riveted tightly in its place, then took a grip at the midpoint of the hard-wood shaft where rawhide thongs had been wet-wound and shrunk on to offer a sure hold; with his right hand, he grasped the shaft about halfway between the midpoint and the horn-shot butt of the spearshaft. Then he began his cautious advance on the outré beast, erect, but with his knees slightly flexed, moving on the balls of his feet, ready to jump or shift suddenly in any direction necessary.

The well-trained dogs had drawn back from the attack, but they still half-crouched, one on either side of the wounded predator, just out of easy reach of its slavering jaws. The other four young men had each accepted the loan of an arrow from Bard Herbuht's quiver and now they and he had taken up positions around the killing ground, lest the beast essay to bolt.

Milo could see why the bolas and riatas had not been used by these young warriors who, of all the far-flung Kindred clans, truly excelled in the use of them —this beast was relatively short-legged and went just too close to the ground to be easily snared up in the rawhide ropes.

With a bear, one could often slash a forepaw sufficiently deep with the knife-edge spearblade to cause the ursine to stand erect on the hind legs and give a spearman a clear shot at the heart or throat, but this beast did not look to be of a shape to be able to attack in such a position. Nor did it look to be of the sort that would leap, like a cat, giving a well-coordinated and iron-nerved spearman the opportunity to let the predator impale itself on the spear. No, he thought, this one will come in low to the ground and without a doubt very fast, too; so . . .

He had just set himself to stab at the head of the beast when that toothy head and the rest of the creature lunged at him with what seemed the speed of light. His too-high spearblade just slid across the top of the beast's flat head, slashing only the edge of a black ear, but then he was able to raise the butt and lower the point enough to sink it deeply into the sinewy neck at its confluence with the shoulders.

Putting his weight on the lucky thrust, he held the beast pinned even while he felt the burning agony of sharp teeth tearing through the thick leather of his boots and into the flesh of the leg beneath. That was when Little Djahn Staiklee stepped up and, crouching, buried the five-inch steel head of his spearblade behind the near foreleg of the beast, just below the withers. At the same time, Gy Linsee took a few quick steps and, at a range of two feet, drove an arrow into the right eye of the outsize mustelid.

As soon as the beast's remaining eye began to glaze over in death, Milo drew out his spearhead from its body, thrust it into the earth a couple of times in order to at least partially cleanse it, then paced over to where the Teksikuhn still sat crouched in the grass, grimacing with pain, part of his left trouser leg soaked in blood, his face as colorless as fresh curds where not weather-tanned.

When mindspoken, the boy looked up with pain-filled blue eyes, not releasing, however, his hold on the bowstring-and-stick tourniquet in place high up on his thigh. Shaking his head even as he mindspoke, he beamed back bitterly, "No, Uncle Milo, that critter didn't do me no harm. No, it was that damn fool Bili-Fil come close to killing me! Cast his dart at that whatever-it-is and put the fucker into my leg instead. Sometimes I think my brother is purely set to see ever drop of blood I owns."

With Milo's help, the young man stood and then managed to mount one of the horses. "Gy," said Milo, "get him back up to the camp and tell Djoolya that he took a dart in his thigh. She'll know what to do. Then ride back down here with some more horses, one with a pack saddle; I don't want to stay down here in this grass any longer than absolutely necessary. Another of those things"—he gestured at the arrow- and dart-studded body of the strange beast —"or a whole pack of them could be in one of those patches of the higher grasses and we'd never know it until they chose to show themselves."

Of course, it was not that easy; Milo reflected that it seldom was. The packhorse did not like the smell of the dead beast and refused to go and stay in close proximity of it. The other horses, even the hunters, were no better, and no amount of coaxing or mind-speak soothing by Milo and Gy could achieve equine cooperation. Finally, Gy made yet another trip to the hilltop campsite and came back with one of the big, powerful, gentle mules of the pair that pulled Milo's cart on the march. She snorted her plain disapproval of the stink and stamped a couple of times, but made no other objections to having the furry, blood-soaked thing tied onto her back.

Once back up on the top of the hill, Milo found the yurts all back up and layered. This time they were arranged in a circle with the empty carts parked between them, the whole forming a barrier to the horses the milled around the rest of the hilltop.

The lashings were loosed and the heavy body was dumped from off the mule-mare, then Milo called in all three cats—the two prairiecats and the jaguar—to thoroughly examine and scent-record the beast, beaming, "Remember this smell, all of you. Spotted One, is this beast at all familiar to you?"

"Who could ever forget such a stench, brother of cats?" She wrinkled her nose and shook her head in distaste. "No, if this cat had scented or seen one of these before, even as a cub, she would certainly recall it."

To Djoolya, he beamed, "How is the boy? Is he still bleeding?"

"Not much, now," came back her response. "But even so, I don't think he should fork a horse or even walk around much for a few days, my dear."

"Hmmm. Well, I suppose I could rig a horse litter out of two of the pry-poles, a couple of riatas and a cured hide or two. But knowing these southern Kindred, we'll also have to use a third riata to tie him into that litter, unless you can brew him up a tea to knock him out for the day." Milo shook his head dubiously. "Or do you think we could pad the load of a cart enough to bear him without further injury?"

"You do mean to move on today, then, Milo?" she beamed. "Do you think that best for us?"

He shrugged. "Far better than staying here, I'd say. That high, dense grass surrounding this hill bothers me; it bothered me to begin, but now, combined with that huge, vicious thing we just killed, it has me very worried, and I'd much rather move on to an area where we can at least see more than a bare score of yards out from the camp. True, mustelids are usually solitary beasts, but I have seen pairs of them hunting together here and there and the thought of so much as one more of that ilk"—he waved at the body with the women, children and cats gathered around it and the flies crawling all over it—"sets my nape hairs to twitching."

"So, yes, let's start getting the yurts down and loaded up, the teams harnessed and hitched. Two of the warriors ought to be enough to do for the hurt dogs, two more to go about their yurt and cart. Gy and I and the other one will get the hide off that thing."

Djoolya wrinkled both her brow and her button nose. "Do you think you'll ever get the reek out of that hide, Milo? And even if you do, finally, will it be worth the effort of scraping and curing and then sewing up all the rents and punctures and tears with sinew? If you'll observe, that's a warm-weather pelage, not a thick winter one."

"We always get the muskiness out of mink and fisher and martin and even wolverine, don't we, Djoolya?" he replied. "Does that skunk-skin cap of yours now smell at all like the former owners?

"You're right, of course, about the light fur, but if this beast is as rare a one as it seems to be, it should have value as a novelty, if nothing else, and we might get something of more worth in trade for it, somewhere along the line.

"Oh, by the way, that two-handled gray-steel box from the ruin—where is it now?"

As he squatted at the tail of a canted cart, feeding the fat, stubby, ancient but still shiny .45 caliber cartridges into three of the silvery stainless-steel magazines, Milo felt a brief stab of longing for that world now long centuries in the dead past, that world of which these deadly artifacts were only pitiful reminders.

After he had threaded the webbing magazine pouch onto the pistol belt and hooked the leather holster in place, he cinched it about his waist, inserted a loaded magazine into the butt of the weapon and slipped it into the holster. Even with the holster flap secured, however, he still was worried about the possibility of the irreplaceable pistol falling out, so he snapped the lanyard to the butt ring.

He now half-wished that he had left the way clear to obtain one of those powerful rifles that had been stored with the pistol. That would have put paid to such a big, dangerous animal quickly enough, and from a far safer distance than this pistol, the primary utility of which was and had always been mankilling at very close quarters.

When he at last got around to pulling off the

pierced, torn boot, there was, aside from torn, blood-stiff trouser leg and sock, no mark to show of his injuries inflicted by the creature's sharp teeth and strong jaws and fury, but then he would have been shocked if there had been such. With a deep sigh of annoyance, he sought out his clothing chest and another pair of boots.

Sacred Sun was well up in the sky by the time the party got on the move, so they set a brisk pace, taking only such game as they came across directly in their chosen path, not taking time to actively hunt for prey. Snowbelly ranged out ahead alone, while the other two cats alternately ran the flanks of the column and trailed the horseherd, seeking out any trace of the musky stink that identified the peculiar beasts like the one whose pelt—now scraped and soaked and salted and rolled up—rode along lashed to the tailgate of a cart, dripping water and serum and covered with dust and a metallic-hued carpet of feeding flies.

Pushing onward an hour or more after the usual halting time unexpectedly brought them to the fringes of the ruined city, and, after finding a lake a mile or so north, Milo and the party set about making camp near the lakeshore among the scorched, tumbled, much-overgrown shells of the homes that had apparently composed part of a small subdevelopment, long ago, in another time, in a vanished world.

Milo still was unsure of their exact location. However, he felt they were too far north for the ruined city to be Tulsa; they might be somewhere in western Missouri, but he suspected, rather, southeastern Kansas. With any kind of luck, there should be something left still legible in those ruins to tell him precisely.

He breathed a silent sigh of relief when, after a wide-swinging circuit of the lake area, the cats reported no trace of the scent of the ilk of the giant mustelid, though there seemed to be a plentitude of game and a few of the more normal predators about.

"No lions or big bears, I hope?" queried Milo.

"Not that I sniffed out," replied Snowbelly, adding, "There is a sow bear and her two half-grown cubs denning in a place just east of the camp, but she is not one of the big, flat-faced bears, only one of the smaller, the ones you call black. The only cats about seem to be the short-tailed ones."

"There is at least one bigger cat," Crooktail put in.

"Puma?" Milo asked.

"No, bigger," she replied. "Not so big as me or even as Spotted One, though."

"Maybe just a very big puma, then, cat sister?" beamed Gy Linsee. "They can get big. When my sire was a boy, guarding sheep of a night, he speared and killed a puma that weighed a hundred and fifty pounds."

"No, Brother Gy," Crooktail beamed back. "This cat smells in no way like a puma or like Spotted One, either, although she is just a little smaller than Spotted One and, also like Spotted One, will soon throw cubs."

Milo nodded. "All right, we'll camp in this place tonight only. Tomorrow we'll move farther northeast and put the widest part of the lake between the camp and herd and those ruins.

"Snowbelly, no more than one of you cats is to night-hunt at a time; I want at least two guarding the herd, constantly. With really plentiful game hereabouts, of course, the predators may not exhibit any slightest interest in trying to take a horse at all, but those who take enough chances usually suffer for it in the end.

"Herbuht, you and Djim-Bahb Gahdfree take the hunt in the morning, eh? I'll be taking Gy and Little Djahn over into the main ruins to see what we can see."

It was unnecessary for him to add that they would harvest any edible animals they chanced across—that was simply the Horseclans way.

Like the isolated ruin they had found back west on the prairie, most of the small city was tumbled and thickly overgrown and, under the vegetation, there seemed to be frequent indications of old conflagrations. The three horsemen rode slowly along what once had been . metaled roadways, but now the macadam or concrete only showed through in the rare spot here and there beneath the soil that held the roots of grasses, weeds, shrubs and trees.

Milo led a curcuitous way toward the visible, multistory ruins that he thought to be the center of the dead city. He did this in part because, uneven as was the surface of the streets, occasionally rent or bisected by subsidences of varying widths and depths where subsurface piping had collapsed, still did those streets offer more reliable footing for the horses than might have been obtained by threading a way between the overgrown ruins of homes and smaller buildings that lined them. Another reason for avoiding the tangles of brush and vines was his desire to, if possible, avoid for now the beasts likeliest to be denning within the roofless, sagging walls or the tumbled piles of masonry; he and most of his clans only killed predators when the folk or their stock were threatened by the beasts or when the pelts were needed for clothing, bedding or trade—and this was no season for good pelts to be had.

As they entered upon a street forking off one along which they had been riding, the cawing of carrion crows caused them to look up into a huge-boled, ancient oak. There, some thirty feet up the tree, wedged into a crotch, was the partially eaten carcass of a white-tailed deer. All the hide and flesh were gone from the head and neck, shoulders and forelegs; moreover, the doe had been partially gutted.

"Now how in the hell did that deer get up there, I wonder?" remarked little Djahn Staiklee.

Recalling Africa, Milo said, "She was put up there to keep her out of reach of other meat-eaters until the killer comes back to feed again on her. That little trick answers the question of just what kind of large cat it was that the prairiecats smelled out in these ruins. The only cat of any size that does that is the leopard."

"Leopard, Uncle Milo?" asked Gy Linsee. "What kind of cat is it?"

"Very similar to Spotted One, Gy," he replied. "Spotted, like she is, very strong and agile, very territorial, and unpredictable of temperament, too. They will hunt and kill and eat anything they can catch and pull down . . . including humans, though they seem to prefer prey the size of that doe up there. We'll be wise to avoid her, if possible, especially since she'll soon have cubs to protect and to feed. That she's placed her larder in that particular tree may mean that she's denning close to it, so we'll take another route out of the city and let her be."

After about a quarter mile more of riding, the street debouched into another, much wider one, stretching nearly a hundred feet from one side to the other and lined with wrecked towers of rust and pitted masonry, some featureless fronts, others pierced with regular openings that once had been windows but that now gaped blackly like the eyeholes of bare, picked skulls.

At a distance of ten or twelve feet from the fronts of these ruins lay small, roughly rectangular mounds that Milo could still identify as the rust-eaten hulks of trucks and automobiles. The mere presence of such here meant that this city had never before been visited by the metal-hunters, else they would no longer be standing in one piece.

To young Staiklee, he said, "Here's the answer to your father's problems, Djahn. When we get back to camp, either you or your brother must ride back westward, find your clan and tell your father to bring them east, to this place, if he wants metals. This city looks to have been unvisited by man for a century or more, at least. Clans Staiklee and Gahdfree could mine it, off and on, for years to come, bartering everything they can't themselves use to the traders.

"These hulks alone"—he waved at the remnants of vehicles—"will contain more than enough still-usable steel to outfit every warrior in the two clans with armor and weapons, shoe every last horse and mule and draft ox and still give enough left over to trade off.

"Now, let's dismount and look more closely at some of those ruins. But, Gy, Djahn, stay with me at all times and be very, very cautious—we don't want part of a building to collapse on us this morning."

But most of the easily accessible metal on the building fronts proved to be aluminum extrusion and so badly oxidized as to be very brittle and utterly useless. The first lucky find was in a booth inside the ground-floor lobby of a large building; here they were able to collect and bag several hundred brass key blanks, which, properly ground down and shaped and sharpened, would become as many fine brass arrowheads.

A similar booth in the same building lobby was also a treasure trove of sorts. Once Milo had broken off the rusty lock of the counter cabinet—all of thick, heavy-duty acrylic plastic, now dim, dirty, discolored and slightly warped but still sound—the two younger men wondered and exclaimed at the dozens of knives and daggers of fine steel, along with stones and steels for sharpening.

The next booth yielded a quantity of cups, mugs, bowls and goblets of pewter, silver plate, gold plate and anodized aluminum, keychains and currency clips in assorted metals, a double handful of small charm pendants in sterling silver and an equal or larger number of finger rings of turquoise and German silver as well as several massive silver rings in the forms of skulls, wolf heads, cat heads, goat heads, ram heads, bull heads, Satan heads, and eagle heads.

Within the space of a bare hour, the three men had filled to overflowing the sacks they had brought along on this reconnaissance with artifacts of the civilization that had preceded their own, and Milo suggested that they ride back to camp.

"Nothing we leave is going anywhere in our absence," he remarked jocularly.

On the ride back out of the ruined city, Gy Linsee's flawless archery skills brought down no less than four tiny antelope—each of the creatures not much larger than a big rabbit, and two of them equipped with miniature, but sharp, horns as evidence of their true maturity, despite their size.

"Did you ever before see such little antelopes, Uncle Milo?" asked Gy.

Milo nodded. "Yes, and they were this kind, I think, too, but that was very long ago and very, very far away from here. I believe these were called dikdiks or something similar; like that leopard, they were not originally native to this continent, so there must have been a zoo or preserve or, more likely, a park where animals from other parts of the world were allowed to run loose somewhere around here. That's where the plains lions came from, you know, and all of the antelope with unbranched horns, too."

Once out onto the open prairie, Gy and Djahn Staiklee vied with each other in flushing out and arrowing rabbits, so that they all arrived at the new campsite with the four minuscule antelope, no less than seven plump rabbits and the heavy bags of nonedible booty.

There was already much food in the camp. Bard Herbuht's hunt had chanced across and brought down a good-sized feral heifer only an hour or so out and, on their way back, had found a salt spring whereat they had been able to kill a ringhorn buck.

Moreover, while clearing the new campsite, some clutches of bird eggs had been discovered, and the bard's children had brought in two armadillos. Karee Linsee had found an extensive stand of sunflowers and had dug up nearly a bushel of the thick, tasty roots. Not to be outdone by Gy's other wife, Myrah Linsee had strung her fine bow, taken a fishing arrow or two, a spool of line and a few crickets, and repaired to the lakeshore, returning with three good-sized bass and a catfish.

There seemed to be a plenitude of firewood, for a change. Nearby was an entire stand of trees that apparently had been drowned in some unusual rise of the lake's water level, years agone. Dried by years of the constant prairie winds, the numbers still standing were become excellent fuel, and given the frugal ways of Horseclansfolk, there was enough wood to last the small encampment's needs for months.

Milo was inordinately pleased. With so much food on hand, there would be no need to mount any hunt on the morrow, so he could take a couple of carts, the experienced Djoolya and all but a couple of the young warriors back with him and Gy to the ruined city center with all the tools they would need to delve more deeply and thoroughly. Bard Herbuht could and willingly would remain in charge of the camp.

When they had finished the heavy meal and still were all sitting around the central firepit, Gy Linsee spoke. "Uncle Milo, on the hunt you led last fall, you let us into your memories, that we all might learn of how things were in that other world, that world which gave birth to the Sacred Ancestors. But you never allowed us, then, to know all of it—you closed your memories one night after we had learned of your return from a long, terrible war.

"Uncle Milo, I would know the rest of that tale. I would know of how folks lived in those times. I would know of your life, too, in that strange world, teeming with people."

Milo nodded. "Yes, I recall my promise to you, Gy. I did tell you that if you came with me and Bard Herbuht, I would either tell you the rest of the tale or let you into my memories. I will. We'll start this night, and since all here are mindspeakers, there will be no need to talk myself hoarse."

Then he opened his memories.

Chapter II

Five persons accompanied Brigadier General Eustace Barstow back to the United States—Major Milo Moray, Captain Sam Jonas, First Lieutenant Karl Metz (Padre), First Lieutenant Eli Huber (Buck) and Second Lieutenant Elizabeth O'Daley (Betty). Arrived at their destination, Fort Holabird, Maryland, they stayed only a few days, the five of them restricted, under direct orders not to write anyone, telephone anyone, or try to leave the small post for any reason.

While the group were lounging in the officers' club one early evening, Milo heard a nasal, vaguely familiar voice, let his gaze rove around the room and spotted a pasty, vaguely familiar, face of a captain who was both talking and assiduously gnawing on his nails. After a moment of thought, he placed the voice and the face and hung the proper name upon them. Without another word to his companions, he stood up, pulled his Ike jacket down and straight, then paced deliberately across the shiny floor.

He came to a halt directly in front of the nail-biting officer, clicked his heels together smartly and said, "*Guten Abend, mein Herr Sturmbannführer* Jarvis. How is it that you're still wandering around loose without a straitjacket? Remember me? I'm Milo Moray."

The wan man became even paler, and his muddy-brown eyes widened and his jaw went slack, revealing to Milo that he looked to have not brushed his stained, crooked teeth since last they had met back at Fort Benning years before. His lips finally began to move, but no sounds came from him for a few moments.

Finally, he got wind behind his words. ". . . be impersonating an officer of the Army of the United States of America. You can't be a real officer, simply cannot be! They promised me, swore to me, that you'd never, ever get a commission."

"So," growled Milo, "it was you, eh? You were the one who kept getting my promotion requests blocked."

"Of course I did, Moray, I had to . . . I just had to, and you know why, too. I thought it all out after you had had me reprimanded and demoted. I realized that I had been right about you from the start."

The two officers at an adjoining table, to whom Jarvis had been talking, were clearly puzzled, so Milo stated, "Gentlemen, this man was a major in 1942—CID, I think—I was a Regular, first sergeant of a basic-training company. He waltzed in, found out that I speak a number of languages, and proceeded to accuse me of being some kind of Nazi spy or plant. He caused me a good deal of trouble, but I was proved innocent of his groundless charges and returned to duty; he was brought up on charges, and had it not been for the war and some well-placed friends he had, he would probably have been cashiered, let go for the good of the service. As it was, he was, as he just said, reprimanded and demoted to first lieutenant. This is the first time I've laid eyes on the lunatic since then."

Turning back to Jarvis, he said, "Well, you tin-pot Torquemada, so you still think I'm a Nazi, eh?"

"Oh, no, Moray, not anymore, not for years now,

not since I thought it all out. I know you for what you really are, now, you see. That was why I exacted certain promises from certain friends in high places, you see. I don't know . . . I still don't know just *what* you are. But I do know you're not one of us, that you're not a human being. That's why I knew that I had to do all that I could to deny you power, deny you control over real people, human people, for as long as I could. I did it for humanity, to protect us all from you."

Jarvis turned to the two other officers, tense, intent. "You see, Moray . . . this thing that calls itself Moray . . . it's not really a man at all. It's nonhuman. I know. I sensed it years ago, but now I know, *I know*. Now he . . . it will probably kill me because I know, but when I die, you must know that it will be for you, for you and all the rest of real humanity. Can't *you* see? *Can't any of you see?* He's inhuman . . . no, *un*human. I've seen him in my dreams—and just ask anybody who knows me, sooner or later my dreams all come true— I've seen him walking around in a world where almost all the real human beings are lying dead all around him. All of humanity lying cold and dead, with animals eating their bodies, and him, it, this thing that calls itself Moray, still alive. I've seen it all. I've seen it. You've got to see it! Can't you see it, really?"

Milo admired the restraint and fast thinking of the older of the two officers. "Possibly, Captain Jarvis, if Bill and I were able to talk to this officer, and, uh, examine him outside, in a less noisy place for a while . . . ?" Arising, he said, "Major, would you please walk outside with us briefly?"

In the foyer, the lieutenant colonel sighed and shook his head sadly. "Poor Jarvis—he's never been strung together very tightly, not as long as he's been here, at any rate, and I would venture a layman's opinion that he finally went over the edge this evening. You probably triggered it, Major Moray, but don't feel too bad about it. As I say, it has clearly been coming for a long time."

Milo nodded. "I was told by a psychiatrist who had interviewed Jarvis that the man was, even back in '42, a mental basket case. But I can't say that I'm sorry about bringing on his dissolution, this way. You both heard him say that he had twisted tails to keep me from being commissioned."

"And you believe his babble, major?" asked the younger officer.

"I do, captain, simply because *someone* or *something* kept me a sergeant for most of the war, kept getting commission request after commission request bounced back marked 'disapproved.' The only thing that ever got me commissioned, finally, was combat attrition, and that, well after D-Day. And if those commission requests had not been disapproved, there is a chance that the best friend I ever had would still be alive today. So, no, I'm not in the least sorry if it was my presence, my words, that drove that bastard in there over the edge.

"But what do we do now, colonel?"

The older officer frowned. "Let me make a couple of calls, eh?"

When the captain at last ushered Jarvis out into the foyer, it was emptied of all its usual personnel and any members other than the two captains, the colonel and Milo. Milo's wrists were secured with handcuffs and a brace of hard-eyed military policemen flanked him.

"What . . . ?" began Jarvis.

"There is some reason to suspect that you may be right about this officer, Captain Jarvis," said the colonel, "I want to take him over and let Major Tatian look him over. Maybe he can tell us whether or not he's human. If a surgeon can't, who can, say I. You'll come with us, of course—since you rode the hunt for so long, I feel you should be there when the fox is driven to ground. Let's go."

At the post dispensary, the tired duty officer wasted no time and took no chances. Before Jarvis had stepped more than a few feet beyond the doorsill, there was a big, beefy medical corpsman on either side of him, gently but very firmly gripping his skinny arms with hands the size of hams.

But it did not prove to be that easy, after all. When the third corpsman, smiling and speaking soothing words, began to unbutton Jarvis' uniform blouse and he saw a fourth approaching with a straitjacket, the slight man shrieked and began to resist with an unsuspected strength, flinging the big, strong men about the room like so many rag dolls. It devolved into a brief battle-royal, finally requiring the full efforts of five corpsmen, the surgeon and the two military policemen to immobilize the raving officer long enough to get the straitjacket on his arms and body and some thick webbing straps buckled around his ankles and legs.

After the patient had been borne off and strapped to a bed, someone at last thought to unlock Milo's handcuffs. As he rubbed his wrists, Milo thought that the surgeon had come out of the fracas with the least amount of damage—he would have a hellacious black eye, but that was mild when compared to the injuries of his staff members and the two MPs, most of whom looked as if they had been knocked down and run over by a herd of maddened, stampeding horses.

"God be thanked that I thought to trick him into coming over here," said the colonel with fervor. "Can you imagine what kind of shitstorm a donnybrook like that would've whistled up if it had happened in the O-Club? Thank you, Major Moray. You're one of General Barstow's staff, aren't you?"

"Yes, sir," replied Milo.

The colonel nodded brusquely, "Yes, well, I'll tell him about all this and mention just how much your cooperation helped us."

Turning to the surgeon, who was just then preparing to set the apparently broken arm of one of the MPs, he asked, "Well, Eddie, what'll you do with Jarvis now?"

The medical officer shrugged, then winced, and said, "Hell, we have no facilities for a case like his here, colonel, you know that. Ship him down to the N-P section at Walter Reed, I guess."

Barstow left Holabird for a few days, and upon his return, he and the five officers he had brought from Germany, plus another lieutenant, three sergeants and four privates, departed Holabird in three Army sedans followed by a three-quarter-ton weapons carrier loaded with their duffel bags, B-bags and other luggage.

Milo had, for some reason, assumed that their destination was either the District of Columbia or the area of Virginia just south of the capital, but he was proved wrong. The small convoy slowly threaded its way through the congested traffic of Washington, crossed the Fourteenth Street Bridge and headed south on Route 1.

In addition to the driver, one of the newcome privates, Milo shared the sedan with Lieutenant Eli Huber and the new officer, Lieutenant Vasili Obrenovich. To the new officer, he said, "You know the lay of the land now better than we do. Where do you think we might be going? Belvoir, maybe? We're well past Fort Myer."

"We're now past where we should've turned off this highway for Fort Belvoir, too, sir. I dunno, really. Let's see now. South of here is Camp Hill, but I doubt we'd be going there. The next real post south after that would be Camp Lee. Sorry I can't be more help, sir."

All following the lead automobile, General Barstow's conveyance, the convoyette proceeded on south on Route 1 in the crisp, late-autumn weather, through northern Virginia. Woodbridge fell behind them, then Dumfries, Quantico and Stafford. They passed through Fredericksburg, Thornburg, Ladysmith, Cedar Forks and Doswell. In the sleepy college town of Ashland, the lead vehicle was seen to pull off the road, and the other four faithfully followed.

After a brief consultation with Barstow, Captain Sam Jonas handed the driver of each of the vehicles a five-dollar bill and ordered them to have their vehicles gassed and serviced at the Shell station across the road, then return, park them and join the rest of the party in the restaurant.

"That's damned funny," remarked Lieutenant Obrenovich, with a look of puzzlement.

"What is?" asked Milo.

"The money the captain gave the drivers, sir," Obrenovich replied. "Every movement I've been on, if civilian POL facilities had to be used, they were paid in Army scrip, not in cash. This must be some kind of really hush-hush operation that nobody wants any records of."

Neither he nor any of the others then could have known just how right was his surmise. But they would all live to learn.

All fed and refueled, they headed out south once more. In the city of Richmond, they changed routes and direction, east on Route 60, through Sandston, Roxbury, Providence Forge, Lanexa, Toano, Norge, Lightfoot and on toward Williamsburg.

"Any ideas yet, lieutenant?" asked Milo tiredly.

"Oh, yes sir," was the quick reply. "There's only three places down here we could be going—Camp Eustis is just the other side of Williamsburg, then the

Army Air Corps has an airfield called Langley near a town called Newport News, and of course there's Fortress Monroe, in Hampton. I hope it's Monroe—I've heard that that's a good-duty post."

They pulled off the highway and onto the road to Camp Eustis, but once waved through the main gate, they drove directly to the main motor pool, where all —officers and enlisted, male and female—with the sole exception of Barstow were loaded aboard a deuce-and-a-half truck. Then the tailgate was raised and secured and a thick canvas curtain was lashed tightly across the back opening. They sat on the hard wooden seats, crowded closely with their bags and cases piled on the steel bed between the two benches.

Once they were underway, Captain Sam Jonas said, half shouting in order to be heard above the noise of the big engine, "This is orders. It's felt that we'll be better off not knowing just where we're going, how to get there even. The only one who'll know that, for a while, will be the general; he's in the cab of this truck. No, don't bother to ask me any questions—I don't know any more answers than whatall I've just told you."

As they dismounted after a long, bumpy, exceedingly uncomfortable truck ride, they were given no time to look around, but were ushered into the first floor of a building that looked to Milo's experienced eyes like a wooden barrack with all its windows covered by sheets of tar paper. Inside were a score of folding chairs, a few one-gallon butt cans and one thirty-gallon GI can.

Barstow stood beside a rack of brand-new mops and brooms, facing the door by which they all entered. "Sit down," he ordered brusquely, adding, "This won't take long, then you can start getting situated in the quarters you'll occupy while we're here. Smoke 'em if you've got 'em."

With everyone occupying one of the less than comfortable chairs, Barstow, still standing, said, "First off: where you are; you don't know, you don't need to know and most of you aren't going to know, so don't try to find out. There are no public telephones here, and the few outside lines are and will stay under lock and key. Keep away from them or your ass will be grass. Understand? You may write all the letters you want with the understanding that they'll be thoroughly censored before they go to the place from which they'll be mailed; you'll all be given an address to use for return mail.

"Second point." He ticked off another finger. "And listen damned tight to this—your life could depend on your comprehension of what I'm about to say. You are all restricted to the confines of this cantonment area, no ifs, ands or buts, no exceptions of anybody at any time or for any purpose whatsoever! When you get out of this building, you'll see that there is a twelve-foot chain-link fence topped with triple strands of barbed wire completely surrounding this post. Keep away from it—it's electrified with enough juice to fry you crisp. Eight feet beyond the inner fence is an outer one, and the space in between them is filled with barbed-wire concertinas three feet deep. The gates are as high as the fences and fitted with tamperproof alarms. There are guard towers, manned on a twenty-four-hour basis, with searchlights and machine guns and men who are under orders to use them against any human being who tries to get over those fences—coming or going—or through those gates without authorization, and there are walking sentries and jeep patrols, as well as other safeguards that, although you can't see them, are no whit less deadly."

"*Arbeit macht frei*," said Padre bitterly, to no one in particular. Then, to Barstow, "And just how long have you sentenced us all to your private little—

most likely, highly illegal—concentration camp, general?"

Barstow merely shrugged. "Call it what you wish, Lieutenant Metz. It wasn't my idea . . . well, at least not all of it, anyway. Very tight security is needed for this relatively short but urgently vital operation, and this is the only way of which we know to maintain such a state of full security at all times."

"*Security?* Security from who, from what, general?" Padre yelped. "Japan has surrendered now, the Nazis were finished last May, so just who is there any longer to keep secrets from? Or do I really need to ask that of a quasi-Fascist reactionary like you?"

Barstow sighed and shook his head. "I'd think that even a mind as dense as yours would have by now absorbed the fact that you can't anger me with your radicalism and holier-than-thou condescension, Padre. Why do you keep trying, huh? The security measures are, of course, to protect this operation from Uncle Joe Stalin's Russians, the people we'll have to fight in the next war.

"That's enough, Padre, no more of your questions, if that's what they really are. We've had a long, hard trip today, and most of us would like to chow down and get in some sack time—I know I would—and we won't do either until this briefing is done.

"As of work call tomorrow morning, the only people on post who will be wearing uniforms will be me, Sergeant Baker and Privates Hayes and Lyman, plus the cooks, medical personnel and suchlike who will be keeping us reasonably comfortable and this post operating. The rest of you will all be wearing civvies. Those of you who came from Europe with me are accustomed to this drill, the rest of you now know why you were issued civvies back up at Holabird. And no nonuniformed person will ever be addressed by rank or last name here—those of you who want to choose a name other than your own given name or use a nick-name should give that name to Private Hayes before you leave this building.

"As regards quarters, we have plenty of space allotted us, so you can all have private rooms if you wish, or you may double- or triple- or quadruple-bunk, it's entirely up to you. Of course, some more personnel will be joining us shortly, and we may have to give you all roommates when they arrive." He grinned. "War is hell, they say. By the way, Betty, at least two of the incomings will be female, so you'll be assured of someone to go to the loo with you.

"You'll assemble back here after work call tomorrow morning and we'll take a walking tour of our projected areas of activity, then return for more briefing, in-depth briefing.

"Chow tonight will be C-rations."

There was a concerted groan from his audience.

"They won't kill you, this once." Barstow grinned maliciously. "At least they'll be hot, and there's loaf bread and real coffee to go with them, cold milk, too. The cooks won't get here until tonight, but that means you'll have an A-ration breakfast. And you'll all be pleased to know that these cooks of ours are going to be top-notch, every one of them, hand-picked. You'll also be pleased to know, I'm certain, that as we will have no ranks here, everyone will be considered an officer and will be able to receive a liquor ration.

"This room we're now in will be fitted up as a club, with a bar; upstairs will be the closest thing to a PX—smokes, candy, toiletries, items of civilian clothing, radios, that sort of thing, but no money; you can draw scrip against your pay.

"Now, let's go get moved in. At 1800 hours, come to the mess hall, it's the fourth building to your right from this one. Then I would suggest that we all sack in —although reveille here won't be until oh six hundred, hours, we've got a lot to do and not too awfully much time to do it in."

At his nod to Sam Jonas, standing in the rear, that officer half-shouted, "Atten-*HUT*!"

With a scraping and rattling of the folding chairs, the group arose and were dismissed.

Everyone opted for a private room; privacy for many of them had been rare and precious during the war years. There were three rooms owning private toilets, lavatories and sheet-steel shower stalls, and one was awarded to Betty, the largest already was piled with General Barstow's gear, and they drew high-card for the third; Milo won with the ace of clubs.

He was unpacking his bags into wall and foot lockers when there was a knock on his door. Not even slowing down, he said simply, "Come."

Second Lieutenant Elizabeth O'Daley, WAAC, strode into the room, came to a halt and seemed on the verge of snapping to and saluting before she remembered the reasserted rules of Barstow and forced herself back into an appearance of informality. Betty had come over from the States to Munich by way of England and Paris with then-Colonel Barstow when first he had set up his DP-screening operation there. She was a translator of Slavic languages and looked Slavic, despite her Irish name—big-boned and -breasted, dark-blond with fair, big-pored skin and eyes of a faded blue over wide-spreading cheekbones. She had been a WAAC corporal back then, and Barstow had been bumping her rank up ever since that time.

Holding out a broad, thick hand on the palm of which rested a package of Lucky Strikes, she said, "Milo, I prefer Old Golds, and my ration was these. Would you like to trade?"

Milo smiled and nodded toward the small table, on the top of which reposed the package of C-ration cigarettes, matches, field toilet paper and chewing gum. "Sure, Betty. I have no particular preference in smokes. Cigarettes are cigarettes, so far as I'm concerned."

Sighing deeply, her big, heavy breasts rising and falling, she picked up the Old Golds and laid the package of Luckies in their place. *"Gott sie dankt!* You and I are the only two who didn't get Camels, you know, and I can't abide those so-called cigarettes; I've heard that the company makes them of what they sweep up off the cigarette-factory floor at the end of the day . . . and I can believe it. When I buy them, I get Fatimas, but they don't pack those in C-rations, not ever."

He shrugged. "Betty, I learned to smoke whatever came my way a long time ago. But move those things off the chair and sit down for a minute."

When he had lit her cigarette and his own with his Zippo, he took a puff, then said, "You rode down from Holabird with Barstow, didn't you? Yes, so tell me, do you have any idea why we're here, wherever we are? Any idea just what we're going to be doing?"

After exhaling twin streams of bluish smoke from her nostrils, Betty shook her head. "No, not really, Milo. The general is a very private man, you know, when he wants to be. All that I can say is that whatever it is, he considers it to be damned important, to him, to the Army and to the country. On the basis of my knowledge of the man—and I've worked under his command for almost three years, now, ever since the Army found out I could speak and read and write four languages, plus English—I'd say that his attitude means that whatever we're going to be doing will be of vital importance."

"And that's all you know, huh?" probed Milo. "You didn't hear anything the whole trip?"

"Well . . . now that you mention it, Milo. See, I was in the back seat beside the general with Padre up front with the driver until we stopped for lunch, and almost the entire morning was devoted to one of their endless debates. The driver was a Volga German who had, he told me at lunch, lost numerous relatives in the Revolution and the various purges since, and I thought on several occasions he was going to just run that damned Cadillac off the road when Padre came out with certain of his incredibly naive stupidities. You know, Milo, I think that that priest honestly and truly believes that Premier Josef Stalin and Pope Pius XII are just alike."

He shrugged again, tamping out his cigarette against the side of the butt can. "They may well be, from all I've heard, Betty. You must remember, both of them played footsie with Schickelgruber and Company until he fucked them over. Uh, sorry about that, but . . ."

She just grinned. "Don't worry, Milo. WAACs use it too—it's the most-used word in the Army, I think. But do you really think that? Do you really think the Pope and Stalin are conspiring to take over the world, like Padre says? I've just always thought he had a few screws loose, myself."

Milo grunted. "I'm quite certain he does, Betty, and considerably more than just a few. I know a little more about that man than you possibly do. I knew him back before the war, in Chicago, and he was as good as a Nazi then, tied in with the Bund. He and an older priest, one Father Rüstung, caused me a lot of trouble because I refused to get myself tricked into a marriage to a Norwegian-American woman who finally admitted that she was after the couple of thousand dollars I then had, not me. Even so, faced with the facts, finally, those damned priests gave me the bitter and unfair choice of marrying the conniving bitch or being jailed for fornication; that was when and why I left Chicago and enlisted in the Army."

"Well, I'll be damned," said Betty. "I'd never have guessed you for a fellow Midwesterner. You sure as hell don't talk like one. Chicago is where my family settled, too, you know."

"Yes." He nodded. "I knew a lot of Irish in Chicago, lived with an Irish family, in fact."

"Oh, I'm not Irish, Milo, not by birth. O'Daley was my husband's name. My maiden name was Elizaveta Petrovna Dzerzhinski."

"That explains it," said Milo. "You don't look at all to be racially Irish—I'd thought you were some kind of Slav, all along. So you're Russian, eh?"

Pursing her lips, she nodded. "In a manner of speaking, though if my father ever heard me say it, I'd be in danger of getting knocked the length of a room. He's a Rostov Cossack and inordinately proud of the fact. He was badly wounded in the Great War, but despite being crippled, he still raised a regiment to fight against the Reds and he led them until there was nothing left to fight with or to lead, then he got himself and my mother and my older brother, Piotr, out of Russia and into Rumania, where I was born just before we all came to this country. My two younger brothers and our baby sister, Astrita, are all American-born."

Hesitantly, Milo asked, "You said that your husband's name *was* O'Daley. Are you a widow, then, or divorced?"

She sighed and sadly answered, "James was a Fleet Marine. We were married on the sixth of December, 1941, the day after my twenty-first birthday and his twenty-fourth. We had not been married even six months when he was killed, went down with his tor-pedoed ship. I mourned him for about a month, then I enlisted in the WAACs to free a man from Stateside duty to go over and avenge James O'Daley for me." She sighed again and went on. "Papa tried to get into the Army, the Marines, the Navy and even the Coast Guard, but of course he was far too old and crippled, too. Piotr was exempted from the draft because he was felt to be more use to the country helping Papa to run our factory in Gary, Indiana, which was working on defense-industry contracts. Poor little Ivan died at Tarawa, and Sergei lost the foot and lower half of his leg after being wounded in Le Muy, in southern France."

"You've had a rough go of it, haven't you, Betty," Milo stated with patent feeling.

"No, not really, Milo, not as bad as some, my in-laws, for an example. They lost five out of seven children in the war, all sons, all Marines. And the one son who did survive it was, I'm told, so savagely beaten by the goddamn Japs in prison camps that he'll be crippled for life in both body and mind, and never able to come home or even leave the hospital.

"Mr. and Mrs. O'Daley have never stopped mourning any of their boys, and I don't think they ever will until the day they die. But me, I learned to handle my grief for James and Ivan and my brothers-in-law; yes, they're dead and I miss them terribly, but I'm still alive and I must try to make a good life for myself in a world without any of them, and I'm not at all inclined to handle my losses the way that my sister-in-law, Moira O'Daley, did—Holy Orders don't have any appeal for me."

"Yes, you've made a good adjustment, Betty, even I can see that." Milo nodded. "I know just how hard it is, too, to make that kind of adjustment, for I lost a hell of a lot of friends in the war, too. And right at the very tag end of it all, the best and oldest pal I had died in my arms on the street of a small town in Germany, shot by a little kid who couldn't have been as much as fourteen years old, a fucking Hitler Jugend. And my buddy was only there because he had driven out of his way to see me and spend a few minutes with me." The last words contained ill-concealed bitterness.

Betty arose and walked the few steps to reseat herself beside him on the clothes-littered bunk. Laying a hand upon his, she said, "Oh, Milo, that must have been especially crushing for you. But you must not blame yourself for his death. Such cruel things happen in any war. Why, my papa . . . ."

Through the wide-opened door came Padre. "Well," he smirked nastily, "you work fast, don't you, Major Moray? I wonder just what our Fascist General Barstow will have to say about this. Let me warn you, Lieutenant O'Daley, this man is an infamous libertine, a seducer of innocent young womanhood, who still is wanted, I would assume, in the State of Illinois, for the felonious crime of fornication! Even being in close proximity and alone with such a man could imperil your immortal soul, I warn you as a priest of God."

Betty looked at the officious man as if he had but just crawled from beneath a rock. "Padre, please credit both Milo and me with a little intelligence. Had either of us intended to copulate here and now, don't you think we would at least have closed the door, if not locked it? And contrary to what you seemingly have believed for as long as you've served under Barstow, he and I are not and have never been lovers, only friends and companions who share many of the same likes, dislikes and viewpoints."

"So *you* say." The priest sneered. "But I wonder what Barstow will say when I tell him . . . if I tell him."

"Probably," said Milo in a tightly controlled voice, "to keep your sewer mouth shut and your gutter thoughts to yourself, and to mind your own fucking business, knowing him.

"Now, what *I* am telling you is this. You entered my room without leave, Lieutenant Metz. You have just slandered me and cast aspersions upon the virtue of Lieutenant O'Daley here, and the bald fact that if you stir shit it stinks worse than if you don't is the one and only reason that I don't take all this to the general and see if he won't have you court-martialed. I think I should, but I won't.

"However, ranks and insubordination aside"—he stood up, and Padre flinched and took a step backward —"if you are not out of this room and into your own by the time I reach that door . . ." He took but one step forward, glowering, his fists clenched at his sides. And the priest turned and scuttled out of the room and down the length of the corridor like a frightened rat. Milo waited until he saw and heard the priest's door close and lock, then he closed his own and leaned against it, mopping his brow with the sleeve of his shirt.

"I'm glad as hell that bastard skedaddled like that. Mad as I was, I might've killed the little fucker."

She shook out another cigarette and lit it with his Zippo. "Well, no one ever would've known it, Milo. You gave every appearance of being completely cool, calm and collected, so far as I could see. But you know that Padre's not going to keep his mouth shut, don't you? By noon tomorrow, if not before, all of the rest will have had a chance to hear his version of our public orgy in here tonight. Do you have anything to drink, by chance?"

He nodded. "Sure I do, Betty. Sorry, I should've offered before all of this." He delved into the depths of his B-bag and drew out a bottle. "Cognac okay?"

She smiled. "Cognac will be marvelous, Milo—anything but that godawful so-called schnapps we used to get in München. I had to stop drinking it, you know."

Straightening up with the only cup he had been able to find, a canteen cup, he inquired, "Oh, really? Why? Did it really make you that sick?"

Betty laughed throatily. "No, not at all—it was just that I was starting to grow hair on my chest."

He drew the cork, splashed a generous measure into the cup and passed it to her. After a long draft, she lowered the cup, her blue eyes tearing a little.

"Milo," she said huskily, "lock the door and wedge the chairback under the knob, huh?" To his look of astonishment, she added, "If we're going to have the name—and we are when that Padre gets done lying and exaggerating—we might as well have the game. So please lock the door and cut out the light and then please, please make love to me."

Chapter III

"How long ago did all of this happen, Milo, my love?"
asked Djoolya aloud.

Closing off his memories for the moment, Milo
thought, wrinkling up his forehead in concentration.
"Above two hundred winters. Why?"

She chuckled and squeezed his thigh where he sat
cross-legged beside her. "You've not changed a bit,
that's why. I can empathize with that woman, Beti,
though I wonder too why she waited so long to have
you. I wanted you the first time I ever saw you,
wanted you on me, in me, your hands kneading my
flesh. And it's never changed over our years together, I
still want you. She showed good taste, that Beti. But
I'm sorry, let us back into your memories."

Milo awakened to the insistent rattling of the door-
knob, followed immediately by a soft, subdued knocking on the door itself. Cursing under his breath, he
found the Zippo by feel, flicked it open, spun the
wheel and looked at his watch by the light. It was
0545, a dark and unholy hour. Betty lay snuggled
beside him, pressed closely on the narrow bunk; both
were nude under the muslin sheets and GI blankets.

He shook her awake and whispered into her ear,

"There's someone at the door. When I turn on the light you grab your things and hotfoot it into the bathroom and close the door . . . but *quietly*. Hear me?"

He felt her nod in the darkness, then swung his legs out of bed with a somewhat louder curse as his bare soles came into contact with the ice-cold linoleum. Passing his extended arm back and forth in the stygian room, he finally found the chain, pulled it, and the bare bulb set in the ceiling blazed into life.

While Betty bundled her clothing and shoes into her arms and scurried into the private bath, Milo said just loudly enough for a person on the other side of the door to hear, "Hang on, let me get into my skivvies, at least. Who is it, anyway?"

An equally low-pitched voice came from the corridor. "It's Barstow, Milo. Take your time, get decent, but I've got to speak to you before oh six hundred."

When the bathroom door was shut, he padded over to the door, removed the chair from under the knob as quietly as possible, then unlocked and opened it to face a fully dressed General Barstow, who came in and said, "Shut it and lock it again, please."

Spying the bottle and the canteen cup on the floor beside the bunk, he strode over, picked up them both and helped himself to a measure of the pale liquor. "Whew! Thank you, Milo. I needed that. Sam Jonas and I worked until after midnight trying to get the office and umpteen cases of files and records in some semblance of order. And no sooner did I get into my room here and start to unpack enough to go to bed than Padre came knocking on my door with some yarn about how you were a wanted felon from Chicago and he had caught you petting with Betty."

Milo sighed, then said, "General, I was accused of fornication—which is a felony, they said, in Chicago —back well before the war. There was no trial; I left town. Yes, I had coupled with a woman who was well above the age of consent and knew exactly what she was doing. No, Betty and I were not petting when Padre came in here. We were sitting, sharing cigarettes and talking. That man has a very dirty mind, not to mention a big mouth."

Barstow dragged over the chair and straddled it, resting his arms on its back, the canteen cup still in one hand, an unlit cigar in the other. Dipping the mouth end of the cigar into the contents of the cup, he swirled it around for a moment, then jammed it between his big teeth.

"Look, Milo, I don't give a damn what my people do during their off-duty hours—drink, screw, read dirty books, write them, smoke hashish or opium, bugger little boys or pull the wings off flies—just so long as a good job of work is done for me and Uncle Sam during duty hours, see. I don't like Padre, I never have and I doubt I ever will. I only keep the pinko faggot around to keep an eye on him, make certain he doesn't get a promotion or any real power over normal people and because I enjoy verbally abusing him whenever I'm bored.

"I know that you and Betty spent the night together, so don't bother trying to tell me a gentlemanly lie, huh? She's not in her room and she's not in the main latrine, either, she's in your bath, Milo. I'm very glad that you thought enough of her to try to protect her, but there's no need, never was, I approve. You both have had a damned hard war these last few years, and you'll probably be good for each other for a while, even if this relationship never goes any farther than the occasional boff.

"But just thank your lucky stars, the both of you, that this has happened when and where it has—on a very small post, with a post commander who thinks a majority of the Army regs were drawn up by morons for cretins. You'll likely get more flak from Padre and some measure of ribbing from the others, too; how you handle that is up to you, unless physical violence arises out of it, and then I'll have to come down on you, so be warned. You and Betty are welcome to terrify Padre all you wish—and it won't be hard, he scares easily—you can even hurt him a little, just so long as what you do to him leaves no marks and you don't do it before witnesses."

Removing the cigar from his mouth, he drained the cup and tossed it onto the rumpled bunk. After replacing the cigar, he stood up and stepped over to the door. He unlocked it and then, with his hand on the knob, said, "One last thing, Milo. For Pete's sake, don't either of you make the cardinal error of screwing up a good love affair by getting married. I made that mistake once and I've regretted it ever since. If you don't marry, you'll both have good, warm memories of each other as long as you live; if you do, you'll spend the rest of your lives trying to get the bad taste out of your mouths."

Within the succeeding two weeks, a few more personnel were added to their thin ranks. The first three were clearly real civilians, all older men, who kept mostly to themselves, chatting in German in a way that suggested practice of a language for long unused. Then came a man that Milo had not seen since his days at Benning. Emil Schrader looked far older than Milo recalled him. He had a silver bar on each shoulder, a slight limp, and some very impressive ribbons and badges on his chest—Combat Infantry-man Badge, Airborne Wings, Purple Heart with no less than three oak-leaf clusters, Bronze Star, Silver Star and a Presidential Unit Citation.

As soon as the two were done pumping each other's hands and back-slapping, Milo stood back and pointed at the collection. "What the hell, Emil, did you try to win the fucking war single-handed or something? No wonder they were so long giving me anything for a fucking souvenir of my fun-filled tour of Europe Beautiful—the bastards had given all of the available supply to you!

"But how in God's name did you wind up here, Emil? Or am I allowed to know?"

It was not until Schrader smiled that Milo realized that one of the younger man's eyes was not his—a very good color match for the real, remaining one, but a prosthetic, nonetheless—and when he noticed that, he then noticed the faint, well-sanded facial scars, too. The poor little fucker had really had the course, it would seem.

"You're one of the principal reasons I'm here, you know, Milo. After I was released from the hospital three months back, I was given orders to report to Fort Holabird immediately, not even given time for a convalescent leave to go back home to Kansas. When I got there, who should be waiting but that same son of a bitch tried to have me railroaded at Benning, Jay Jarvis. The fucker got me into his office and told me he was going to put me into a tedious, boring, dead-end job there and keep me at it forever, that I'd stay there until I had a long white beard unless I gave him, in writing, a confession that I'd been a Nazi sympathizer before the war and a Nazi agent during the war. He said that he could keep me from getting anything worse than a dishonorable discharge, but that he had to have that statement and that I wouldn't get a discharge of any kind until I'd given him what he wanted.

"Well, hell, Milo, you know damned good and well that I'm just as stubborn as any other fucker and I would've seen hell freeze over solid before I'd've knuckled under to that peckerhead cocksucker. So I've just been sitting up there, marking time, counting paperclips and suchlike with Jarvis harassing me till he was blue in the face, and then you came along.

"So, after they'd shipped Jarvis off to the funny farm to do his OJT in paper-doll production, somebody went through his office files, found out I was there on post doing little or nothing and started looking for a slot for me to fill. They must've looked in my 201 and decided to make a translator or something like that of me, 'cause I was questioned at some length in German—Hochdeutsch, Plattdeutsch, Schweizer-deutsch, the works. A couple days later, they cut orders on me to come to something called Operation Newhaven. And I guess this hashup must be it, huh?"

Milo could but wonder at just why and how the Army had for so long retained Jarvis in a position of some power despite his long-proven lunacy. The arrogance of taking a highly decorated combat officer, fresh out of hospital, still showing the scars and cripplings of hard, faithful service, and employing mental torture on him in order to try to force him to confess to untruths about himself smacked more of the Axis countries or Russia than it did of the United States of America. Jay Jarvis' friends must be very highly placed and powerful indeed to have managed to keep their boy out of a booby hatch for so long a time.

"So," asked Schrader, "if this is Operation New-haven, what does it do that's so hush-hush they won't even let you know where the hell it and you are, Milo?"

"You reported to the general?" Milo answered the question with questions. "What did he have to say to you about your duties here, Emil?"

Schrader shook his head. "That was the quickest I ever got to see any general officer—or any field-grade officer, for that matter, outside of actual combat—in my life. General Barstow was very nice, very friendly, he seemed honestly glad to have me here . . . and he did not say one fucking thing that told me anything about this Operation Newhaven at all, just warned me that I'd get fried on the wire or my ass shot off by the guards if I tried to get out without somebody's say-so, said I'd learn more in due time, then he turned me over to a Captain Jonas. Sam chatted with me for a while, then turned me over to a Sergeant Quales, who took me to the back of the building, issued me an armload of civilian clothes and shoes, dumped them all in a brand-spanking-new foot locker and told me it would be brought to my quarters later. Then a Lieutenant Obrenovich took over and took me over to the BOQ and told me which rooms were already taken and which building to come to after I'd gotten my gear more or less squared away. And I repeat, what the hell is this Operation Newhaven, anyhow, Milo?"

Milo chuckled. "You have been told exactly as much as Barstow has told any of the rest of us, Emil, and we've been here two-three weeks, most of us, too. How did they get you down here from Holabird, car?"

Schrader shook his head once more. "Naw, Milo. They drove me to some little bitsy airfield and put me and my gear on a Piper Cub—you know, like they use to spot targets for the artillery—a two-seater and flown by an enlisted pilot who had about as much to say as a stuffed owl. We landed at an Air Corps place called Langley and me and my gear got put into the back of a half-ton GI panel truck with the back windows painted over—both sides of the fucking glass, too, for shit's sake!—and a fucking plywood partition between the back and the front. When it finally stopped and they opened the back door, it was clear we was on an Army post, but don't ask me where or which one, 'cause they stuck me and my stuff into the back of a three-quarter-ton weapons carrier, tied the back curtain down and took off. Felt like the fuckers were driving cross-country, part of the time, and when they stopped and told me I could get out, it was here, wherever here is."

Four more of the Munich bunch filtered in—Hugo, Ned, Judy and Annemarie—in the same traveling party with a short section of WAAC's under the command of a six-foot-tall Wagnerian blond sergeant named Hilda Stupsnasig. With his well-honed sense of humor, General Barstow immediately dubbed the WAAC sergeant "Brunhild," but simply as an in-joke, since all the WAACs were clerical personnel and as such would work in uniform in various capacities and offices.

At last, Barstow called a meeting of ten of his people —Milo, Buck, Betty, Hugo, Ned, Judy, Vasili and the three older civilian men—in the small conference room behind his office.

"All right, ladies and gentlemen," he began. "Our work, what we all came here for, will be starting day after tomorrow. It's going to be, in many ways, very much like what most of us here were doing in Munich, earlier this year. The difference is going to be that very few if any of the people we are going to be interviewing are DPs. On the contrary, almost all of them are going to be Germans, many of them having had ties of some sort to one of the armed services and/or to various *Staatsbüroen* of the Third Reich, and even those few who will not be Germans will have worked closely with certain German projects which employed the others, the actual Germans.

"These three distinguished gentlemen"—he indicated the three civilians, seated side by side as always since their arrival, all puffing away at their pipes— "will be called Smith, Jones and Doe, and one of them will be a member of each of the three interrogation teams. Buck, you and Judy will be teamed with Doe. Hugo, you and Ned with Jones. You two teams will be dealing only with Germans.

"Milo, you and Betty and Vasili will, with Smith, handle all of the non-Germanic subjects. You, Milo, will also be in charge of all three teams, the facility and so forth. You'll probably need an exec to take some of the load off. You can have any officer not presently in this room. Who do you want?"

"How about Emil Schrader, general?" replied Milo quickly. "He and I worked together years ago. I was a first sergeant and he was my field first; he's a good man."

Barstow nodded. "So be it. You've got him as of now. It'll be up to you to brief him, though. He's a good choice for this, too, come to think of it, Milo. He speaks excellent German and can be used to fill in on either Team One or Team Two in a pinch.

"You ten and Schrader had better go back to the BOQ and pack up. You'll all be moving this afternoon to the small compound on the other side of the post; it's that facility of which you will have charge, Milo. You'll have our own Brunhild and four of her WAACs for your headquarters staff, plus Schrader, of course. There's a small mess hall and hot food will be trucked in to you three times each day, but keeping the place and the trays clean will be up to you and your WAACs.

"This all is being done this way solely for the purpose of isolating you and your interviewees, of making damned certain that as few people here ever see them as possible. They'll be brought into your compound in sealed transport and they'll leave in exactly the same way. Under no circumstances are any of them to leave that compound at any time until you have finished with them."

"Uhh, sir . . ." said Betty hesitantly. "What about a medical emergency? What happens then?"

Barstow nodded once. "A very good point, Betty. In such a case, whatever the hour, you will ring me up and *I* will send or bring personnel appropriate to the situation you describe from the dispensary, out here."

"What kind of billets are we drawing, sir?" asked the woman called Judy.

Barstow nodded again. "There's an old CCC-type barrack building with a detached latrine that the WAACs will have, and another which will house your subjects. There is one three-bedroom bungalow that will be the billet of the three doctors and two-bedroom ones for the rest of you; how you pair off is your business."

"Are we all going to be locked up day and night in that compound, too, general?" Hugo demanded in his thick Westphalian accent.

Barstow shook his head. "No, not at all, Hugo. Milo, Schrader and Sergeant Stupsnasig will have keys to the gate and to the control box for the fence power. The compound is designed more with the aim of keeping unauthorized people out of it than of keeping you all in. But, Hugo, and all the rest of you, too, hear me and hear me well. No one of you will have firearms, while the outside guards will have them, along with the orders to use them should any person try to go over or under or through the wire or the gate. This is no makework we're doing here, it is an operation of earthshaking importance to the Army, the nation and the world."

Barstow's voice had risen, become quite adamant, as he spoke the last sentence. Now he lowered his speaking voice. "There are going to be, as I said, similarities in the conduct of this operation to our previous operation in Munich, but there are going to be glaring dissimilarities, too. In Munich, one of our primary functions was that of finding out, of unmasking, former SS, members of the Nazi Party, bureaucrats, non-German collaborators and the like who were trying to pass themselves off as innocent, abused displaced persons.

"In this operation, on the other hand, it will not be up to any of the military interviewers to make value judgments on the interviewees. The doctors, alone, will make the decisions as to just how useful the individuals will be, and their decisions will be all based upon other things than the politics or the former military activities or affiliations of the subjects in question.

"Those of you who were combat officers or active operatives with General Donovan may dislike some of our new subjects instantly, on first meeting, subconsciously recognizing them as the Enemy. But you all are just going to have to force your conscious to override your subconscious, for the old war is done and now a new one has begun for our nation, our way of life, and, like it or not, these subjects will be allies in this new war, potentially very valuable allies indeed, and they must at all times be treated as such, no matter how they may have behaved in the past, how they behave now or how you may feel about them and their past deeds, gutwise."

"In other, plainer words, general," said the man called Buck, dryly, "you are setting us up here to coddle and kowtow to a passel of Nazi and quisling war criminals, right? Men who would likely be, rightly be, shot or hung or at least imprisoned did they remain in Europe, right?"

Barstow shook his head. "You're not very good at following orders, Buck, are you? Didn't I just say that none of you are to make any value judgments based upon the supposed deeds or misdeeds of our incoming subjects? You've been with me for some time, and, frankly, I'd expected more professional conduct from you.

"I reiterate, ladies and gentlemen: the Second World War is over, done; the initial skirmishings of the new war are already commencing, but not easily visible yet. The subjects who are coming in to us have the potential, many of them, to be extremely valuable to us, to the United States of America and all other free people everywhere, to be of great help in thwarting or defeating the totalitarian aims of the new enemy.

"It has been said that the art of politics makes for exceedingly strange bedfellows. Well, the art of modern warfare makes for even stranger ones, I assure you all. Believe me, I was shocked, too—shocked to the very core of my being—when my superiors gave me this assignment and told me what my people and I would be doing on this Operation Newhaven, but as I already knew and knew well, the danger, the deadly peril, we all face whether or not we know it, I could immediately grasp the necessity of salving over old prejudices and accepting former enemies as respected allies if not as friends. You, Buck, and all the rest of you must follow my lead and do the same. If any of you feel that you cannot, for whatever reason or none, tell me now and I will replace you before any of the operation has started. Well . . . ?"

Milo and Betty wound up sharing a bungalow with Buck and Judy. Buck was a compact, wiry man a bit under average height, with thin, brown hair and gray eyes flecked with green. Always graceful, he was capable of moving as silently and as swiftly as a cat, in some of his ways reminding Milo of certain of the traits of Jethro Stiles. His English had aspects and sounds of Britain, but his *Hochdeutsch* and his French were both flawless and accentless.

Judy was a little taller than Buck. She was round-faced, rosy-cheeked, with thick hair of a chestnut hue. Her arms and legs were thick, but her body was well proportioned, her teeth white and even and her hazel eyes thick-lashed. In a dirndl, she would have looked the very picture, thought Milo, of a strong, healthy, happy Bavarian peasant woman. And her *Hochdeutsch* was sprinkled well with the accents and idioms of Bavaria and Westphalia.

Milo was certain that Buck and Judy were in love, but theirs was an easygoing, relaxed relationship, with little or no public traces of touchings to advertise their emotional attachment one to the other. Back in Germany, he had not known either of the two of them any better than he had then known Betty. Back in Germany, indeed, Milo had spent the most of his nonduty time alone—reading avidly of both English and German books, anything onto which he had been able to lay hands, sipping schnapps and whisky and cognac and wines, trying to wind down to near-normalcy after the long months of privation, squalor, combat, fear and sudden death. Now he was getting to know these coworkers as housemates and friends.

The work they all were doing with the mostly German interviewees had progressed smoothly to date, sixteen men having passed through their hands thus far—fourteen Germans, one Norwegian and one of Rumanian origin. The three doctors had passed on twelve of these men to whatever came after this Operation Newhaven. Barstow had mentioned in an oblique manner that those not passed on were to be speedily repatriated to whatever internment camps they had originally been plucked from and left to whatever fates their wartime activities had earned them from the victorious allies.

On a night when Milo and Betty and Buck and Judy sat in the parlor of the shared bungalows, chatting and drinking and smoking, three new subjects were occupying the tar-paper barrack, their screenings to begin in the morning. This was the smallest number to arrive to date, and all of this lot were German, or listed themselves as such. Earlier in this evening, the four house mates, along with Emil Schrader and Hugo, had listened for a while to the conversations of the three via the microphones well hidden in the subject barrack and latrine, now they and Schrader sat discussing what the three men had said and the thus-revealed personalities of the men, themselves.

"This Hizinger," asked Milo, "what do you make of him, Emil?"

"Clearly the leader of this bunch. A born leader and accustomed to command, I'd say, too. He may well be a German intellectual, but he's clearly not a civilian one; he walks like a soldier, he talks like a soldier and he behaves like a Prussian officer of the *alte Garde*. He puts me in mind of an SS Panzer officer we captured in southern France—hard as nails, tough-minded and so damned convinced that he was right that nothing would or could ever shake his beliefs. That *Untersturmführer* was from the same part of Germany my own folks came from, too, and after I'd come to talk with him for a while I could almost've come to like him, but then he come to get ahold of a carbine, someway, and shot Lieutenant Mallow and I had to blow his head off with my pistol. I think Hizinger over there is just the same kind of Nazi fanatic."

Milo nodded and turned to the others. "Betty, Buck, Judy?"

"Emil is right," said Betty, "Herr Hizinger has got Nazi and SS written all over him. He seems very intelligent, very voluble and well educated, very precise and methodical, but it's clear that he was no civilian specialist at whatever our three scientists—Smith, Jones and Doe—are interested in; no, he was a military man, all the way, probably from birth. I'd give odds that his real name, his patronymic, has a 'von' preceding it, Milo."

"Yes," agreed Buck. "You know, what I think is that this Hizinger got wind of what was going on and thought he might have the ability to pass himself off as a scientist and thus escape Germany, Europe and his just deserts for whatever he may have done in service to Hitler, the Party and the Fatherland."

While Betty and the others had been talking, Judy had just sat in silence, biting her lips and wringing her hands. Now she spoke. "Look, if anyone here in this room has real reasons for hating and despising the Nazis, it's me. But there is this, too, to be considered and not ever forgotten. Not all Germans were Nazis, not all German soldiers were Nazis, not even all German officers were Nazis. There were even SS men who were not Nazis or even Germans, for that matter. Whether this Hizinger was a scientist or a soldier or both or neither, he deserves to be judged just as objectively as we judged all of the men who came before him and will come after him. If he is a Prussian—and I doubt that he is, he doesn't have that accent—that is not at all his fault. Who has choice in where he is born?

"I do not in the least like this dirty business of listening to the conversations and private acts of our subjects without their knowledge or leave, Milo. Yes, I know, you are going to say that the general says that it is necessary to do such things for the good of the nation, but reflect, if you all will—this is precisely the excuse used by Hitler, Stalin, Mussolini and every other dictator to legalize even the most heinous and unspeakable acts against individuals and groups.

"After this exchange, tonight, I suggest, in the pursuit of being fair and truly objective, that Herr Hizinger be turned over to Team Two. Let Hugo, Ned and Dr. Jones determine his true status-to-be."

The next morning, Milo did turn Hizinger over to Hugo, giving the subject called Faber to Team One and the one called Gries to Team Three, with Emil Schrader filling in for him in his absence. He felt a need to confer with Barstow, not because of what Judy had said as much as because of the way she had said it, and also partially because of things not heard but felt, sensed.

Barstow ushered Milo back into the small window-less, soundproofed conference room, closed and locked the door, and offered Scotch and a cigar. When he had heard it all, he carefully nudged the ash from off the end of his *puro* and raised his bushy eyebrows. "Milo, in any operations of the kinds I've been running, the chance of innocently harboring one or more jokers in the deck is a distinct possibility, but if we do have such here, I don't think Judy is the one. I'm going to tell you why, but what I say is for your ears alone—you don't repeat it to anyone, not even to Betty. *Verstehen?*

"Of course, you've noted how close Buck and Judy are? They've been together for a long time and through particular hell. They're what is left of a team of three people, the third of whom was Judy's husband. They were not really military, they worked for another group and worked in France for quite some time before D-Day and after, successfully pass-ing themselves off as French.

"After the landings, as the Allied armies got closer, Judy's husband must have gotten a little too cocksure. He stayed on the air long enough one night for the Germans to finally triangulate the location of his transmitter. When the Gestapo and Wehrmacht burst in, they caught both Judy and her husband, and very nearly Buck and a member of the underground.

"At that particular time, Milo, maquis units were shooting German soldiers in the countryside and underground types were doing the same thing in the very streets of Paris while the German Occupation Command was debating just how and when to start to demolish Paris as ordered by Hitler himself. The German forces at the front were fighting like hell and still getting pushed farther and farther back, day by day. In that aura of pessimism and facing the specter of approaching defeat, the Gestapo was become exceedingly vicious, frantic to obtain information that might help to briefly stave off or even slow down Armageddon.

"The things that were done first to Judy's husband, then to Judy herself, were unprintable, unspeakable, almost unthinkable to any sane, normal human being. Townspeople said that their screams could be heard even through the five-foot-thick stone walls of the seventeenth-century building the Gestapo was using for a headquarters and prison in that area.

"By the time Buck had gotten together enough men and arms, ammo and explosives, to blast his way into that complex and, after killing a number of Germans, rescue them, Judy was the only one left alive, and she was in a bad way.

"Two days later, elements of the American Second Army liberated the town and Judy was flown to a hospital in England. Buck went back to England, too, but only long enough to be teamed up with some new people and gotten into still-occupied Elsass—Alsace, as the French call it. I understand that they did a bang-up job there, too. Buck was recommended to me when the München operation was first being planned at SHAEF, in England. When I offered him a slot, he told me flat out that he would only come with me if Judy came with him, and I've yet to have reason to regret that I took them both on.

"As you've accurately guessed, Judy is a German. Although her family were aristocrats, the Great War transformed them into what we Americans would call 'genteel poor.' In her teens, she met and married the son of a wealthy, titled English house while the young man was pursuing a course of study at one of the great German universities. Despite the unholy, sophisticated barbarities committed by Gestapo perverts upon her and her late husband, Judy still is proud to be a German, and in light of the truly stupendous fight that Germany put up against impossible odds—a little country of only some sixty million people, total, taking on half the world . . . and nearly winning!—I can't blame her. I'd guess that her outburst last night was simply an upswelling surge of national pride, Milo, nothing more sinister than that.

"So don't worry anymore about Judy, but still keep me informed of any odd or unusual things you notice in the conduct of any of the rest of the group over there.

"And as far as Hizinger is concerned, that's not his name, of course. He was one of Erwin Rommel's favorite young officers. He was ordered back to Germany despite his and Rommel's objections in order to do the other thing he does well, which is said to be a certain realm of higher mathematics. It's considered that if he does agree to work with us, he'll be a real prize."

Outside, in Barstow's office, he pressed a bottle of Scotch and a handful of cigars on Milo, saying, "Don't worry so much, major. You're doing a splendid job. Operation Newhaven is progressing marvelously, and my superiors are very pleased. Didn't I tell you, back in Germany, in München, that if you stuck with me you'dhave a sky's-the-limit future in the Army? By the way, I've already put in paperwork on your lieutenant colonelcy, Milo."

But Milo did continue to worry. He felt a vague sense of unease. And he soon was to find that he had good reason.

Chapter IV

With the dawning of Sacred Sun over the vast prairie, one of the young warriors, Djessee-Kahl Staiklee, set out with several spare horses to search out and bring back Clans Staiklee and Gahdfree to the rich treasure trove of metals that awaited them all in the ruined city of ancient times. He bore written messages from both Little Djahn Staiklee and Uncle Milo, as well as oral urgings from his peers to their own chiefs, sires and siblings.

Of course, he also bore his own eyewitness testimony to the lush verdancy of the well-watered prairie in the proximity of the ruins and of the profusion of the relatively unchary game animals thereabouts. All of these facts would constitute telling arguments in the favor of a movement of both clans, entire—women, children, horses, dogs, cattle, sheep, goats and all—rather than just a party of men to strip what they could from the ruins before rejoining families and moving on.

With plenty of food in camp, Milo took Gy, Djoolya, Little Djahn Staiklee and all but two of the other young warriors back to the ruins, this time with two carts and the proper tools for more thorough delving into those ruins. They hitched up the teams, loaded the carts, mounted and rode out in an icy drizzle borne on a strong but steady wind. However, by the time they came into the far-flung outskirts of the sometime city, the wind had weakened considerably, the drizzle had entirely ceased and Sacred Sun was again peeking here and there through the dissipating cloud cover.

All of the young men had seen other and larger ruins before, of course, for there were many of them athwart the main migration routes that served both wild herds and nomad clans, but all of these had been stripped and picked over years agone. Gy and the young Teksikuhns were awed by the amounts and varieties of the riches of these ruins that had lain for so long untouched.

Milo shooed them all away from the automotive hulks, saying, "Save that scrap metal for the clans to hack apart. The traders give much better barter goods for made artifacts that still are sound and usable. Let's see if we can find a hardware or a farm-supply store."

They found one of each type of store a few blocks south of the tall building area and soon had both carts filled with hand tools, small items of hardware, pots and pans of steel and cast iron and copper, rolls of chain, some galvanized buckets, and two enamelware sets of cups and plates and bowls which caught Djoolya's eye, as too did a large reflector oven. They loaded in yards of verdigrised copper tubing and hundreds of yards of copper wire of various gauges.

Remembering the contents of the sealed fallout shelter cum tomb they had stumbled across out on the prairie, Milo was more than a little relieved to find that sometime in the distant past, the hardware store had been thoroughly stripped of firearms and ammo. Either those same looters or others of a similar bent had taken all of the bows but, strangely, had left behind nearly five dozens of fine bowstrings—individually sealed in plastic and still fresh and usable as they had been on the day they had arrived at the store, at least two centuries before Milo's arrival. He also found a plastic box containing two dozen hunting heads of tempered bronze, the three edges of each still razor-sharp.

Investigation of a small pharmacy showed them evidence of an individual or, more likely, a group interested in drugs and nothing else. The shelves of the prescription section had been stripped absolutely bare and even the nonprescription analgesics were gone, but the remainder of the stock of the pharmacy and the attached variety store was as intact as long, long years of baking heat and freezing cold and the incursions of rodents and insects had left it.

Djoolya came over beaming to show Milo her find of a handful of stainless-steel combs of various sizes, and Milo did not tell her that they had been intended for use on dogs and cats. The nomad woman was also beside herself with joy when she found a small cache of sewing supplies—fine needles, straight and safety pins, assorted buttons, thimbles and a full bucketload of spools of thread in shades and colors the like of which she had never before seen.

One of the rarer finds was that of an entire shelf of quart-size apothecary bottles, vacuum-sealed and containing still-edible dry-roasted peanuts, and just as many pint-sized jars of the same kind filled with cashew nuts or almonds; they could eat the nuts, then trade off the colored-glass jars to the easterners for less fragile merchandise.

Despite the amounts of meat already in camp, the young warriors delightedly vied with each other in knocking over squirrels, hares, rabbits and game birds on the way back to camp. Little Djahn Staiklee took

the pot-hunter prize by neatly smashing the head of a
purplish tom turkey with a shrewd cast of his carven
throwing-stick, just as the tom had lifted from off the
ground, big wings beating furiously. Under those circumstances, a head hit was not even to be expected,
and Milo privately wondered just how much of the kill
had been skill and how much pure, blind, stupid luck,
but aloud, he joined fully in the praise of the young
man's expertise.

Back at the camp, the gleanings were, as usual,
spread out and equally divided among each yurt—
Milo's, Bard Herbuht's, Gy's and that of the young
warriors. Some would go into immediate use of the
nomads, some would be wrought into decorations or
useful purposes, the remainder would be traded off
whenever they crossed the trail of the eastern traders.

The contents of one of the larger jars of peanuts
made an exotic and tasty addition to that night's soup
pot. As soon as the rich soup, the assorted small fowl,
and meat from yesterday's kills and the turkey had
been consumed, Milo was immediately pressed by all
of the others—humans and cats alike—to once more
open his memories that they might hear more of his life
in that strange world of so long ago.

Alone in their shared bungalow bedroom, Milo sat
buffing his cordovan oxfords, while Betty sat at an
improvised vanity table combing her short hair.

"Milo," she asked casually, "the doctors, have they
yet reached any consensus as regards these three
Germans?"

Holding up the shoe and examining it critically,
Milo spat on the toe and once more went at it with the
soft brush. "As a matter of fact, they have. Dr. Smith,
who seems to be their spokesman, came to my office
late this afternoon to give me the results of their
conference. For him, he was quite excited, too. It

seemes that both Hizinger and Gries were connected with the buzz-bomb projects, both the V-1 and the V-2, from almost the beginning until right up to the bitter end."

"And you then telephoned General Barstow with the message, love?" she said, continuing her long, slow, steady brush strokes.

"I tried to, but he was somewhere off post—the girl didn't seem to have any idea when he might be back or where Sam Jonas might be, either. So I guess now it'll have to be morning before I get the info to him and he gets into personal touch with Smith. After that, you know the drill well enough; they'll fuck around with papers and bureaucratic shit for one or two days before the transport finally comes to take this lot to wherever they go from here."

Laying down the brush and turning about to face him, she said, "Good. I will be very glad to see these three go. Valuable scientist or not, this man Gries nauseates me. He never ceases to voice his complaints over the loss of his beautiful estate in the Sandland, the lands and the buildings and the loot from all over Europe with which the main house had been furnished and decorated. The way he goes on with complaint after complaint, one would think that Germany had won, rather than lost, the war."

Milo stopped his buffing and nodded. "I know what you mean. I've heard Gries carry on about his unfair losses. But that damned Faber is the one who gets to me. He's lodged a formal complaint after almost every meal he's eaten here—he apparently expects *haute cuisine* and vintage wines out of an Army messhall. Of the lot, I find that haughty, arrogant bastard Hizinger the easiest to stomach, oddly enough."

She nodded back to him. "I know. That man is dead certain that Hitler is not dead, despite all evidence to the contrary. He makes it abundantly clear that he only is marking time, staying alive long enough to greet and participate in the reborn *Dritten Deutschen Reich*. Even so, he is more admirable a man than that Gries."

"Milo, I'm just as sorry as hell, but I don't know where the general went, where he is now or when he'll be back. He sent me over to Fort Useless yesterday, and while I was gone he took off, no note, no message, no nothing. I think he's trying his level best to worry me into an early grave, that's what I think. But look, if Judy is as sick as you say, I'll have the dispensary send the meat wagon in there and get her to the doc out here; where she goes from there'll have to be up to him. Neither you nor Buck know what might've caused her to start upchucking and running a fever? Something she ate, maybe?"

Milo sighed. "Sam, we all ate the same breakfast. She's the only one who got sick. It could be flu, it could be a virus, it could be some kind of internal problem, hell, it could even be poison, I admit. But if it is, how come nobody else ate it? She can't hold even water down, and with the diarrhea, too, she's going to be dangerously dehydrated in a very short time. I have some few hard-earned medical skills, but administering IV fluids is definitely not one of them, so you'd better get that ambulance in here on the double and get her to somebody who can keep her going."

Back at the bungalow, Buck asked anxiously, "Well, Milo, what's the general say?"

"The general's still not there, not anywhere on the post," said Milo. "But I did talk to Sam Jonas and he's going to send an ambulance from the dispensary to take her back there."

"Thank God for that, at least, Milo, but she needs a real hospital. She's terribly ill—a mere dispensary isn't going to have the facilities to properly care for her."

Milo looked down at the feverish woman, wrapped in a cocoon of GI blankets, her pale face running sweat, hugged up against herself and with her teeth chattering. "Buck, anybody could see that she's in a bad way. Once that surgeon at the dispensary examines her, you know damned well that she'll be on the way to the hospital over at Useless or somewhere. I just pray that whatever she's come down with isn't contagious. That would be all we'd need, in here."

"And I've got to go with her, Milo," said Buck in a no-nonsense tone. "Are you and Sam Jonas going to try to give me flak for that?"

"I'm sure as hell not," declared Milo. "I don't think that the general would, either. He's very fond of her . . . and you, too. As for Sam, well, if there's any flak from him, I'll do the catching of it, Buck. You get cracking and pack what you think the two of you will need in hospital. I'm going back to headquarters and try to type you out an authorization to leave before the meat wagon gets here."

"God bless you, *mon ami*," said Buck humbly. "You are truly a good and caring man." Suddenly he grabbed Milo's hand and kissed the back of it, tears sparkling unshed in his eyes.

Back at headquarters, Emil Schrader was nowhere to be found, and Milo cursed silently; a typist he was not. Cranking the field telephone that connected the various buildings in the small compound, he rang up the WAAC barracks.

A near-baritone voice answered, "WAAC quarters. Staff Sergeant Stupsnasig speaking, sir."

"Sergeant, this is Major Moray. I'm at my office and I need a fast typist, on the double. Can do?"

Milo was surprised at just how fast and accurate a typist the tall, beefy woman was. Her hands, bigger than his own and looking to have been intended for effortlessly crushing granite boulders into powder, handled the Underwood with consummate ease and quickly had the form properly filled out and ready for his signature. He was just signing it when Betty and Hugo strolled in, the two Germans, Hizinger and Gries, with them.

Immediately, Milo detected the air of something being wrong, felt his nape hairs prickle up and an inward sense of deep foreboding. But just then the gate guard unlocked the gate and the boxy field ambulance rolled through into the small compound. Outside the bungalow, Buck waved with both arms, and as the ambulance veered in his direction, he stepped back inside to reemerge with the blanket-swathed form of Judy in his arms, carrying her easily, tenderly.

When the vehicle backed up to the front of the bungalow, a medic hopped out and helped Buck arrange Judy in one of the litters. Then, with the rear doors still flapping open, the ambulance made for the headquarters building to pick up Buck's egress pass.

At the point of two silenced, small-caliber pistols held by Betty and Hugo, Sergeant Stupsnasig had typed and Milo had signed four more passes. Milo was in a state of stunned shock, still barely able to comprehend Betty's duplicity—so warm and loving, even more so than usual only short hours past, now so cold and detached and deadly of demeanor.

The brawny Hugo jerked Buck out of the ambulance with one hand and slammed the side of the silenced pistol against his head with the other. He took a grip on the blankets wrapped around Judy, but then let her go as the two Germans came out of the headquarters building to level his pistol on them while Betty, who had brought them out, turned and reentered, briefly.

"Give me the key to the telephone that connects to

Barstow's office, Milo. Give it to me immediately or
I'll kill you both, here and now."

Milo eased up in his chair, fished a keyring out of his
pocket and dropped it on the desktop. "What the hell
is your game, Betty . . . if that's really your name?
Those passes will get you out of this compound, but
just how do you propose to get out of the main one?"

Picking up the keyring, she half smiled. "We shall
crash through the gate, of course, in the ambulance.
Why else do you think that I poisoned Judy than to get
us an ambulance driver in here?"

He shook his head. "You'll all be fried. That gate has
enough voltage in it to—"

"Please, Milo, spare me. No, we will get through
safely enough. The tires of the ambulance are rubber
and therefore the vehicle will not be grounded. Hugo
explained it all to me."

"The machine gunners—" he began, only to be
again interrupted.

"Those poor, soft-hearted American men will be
most loath to fire on the so-sacred Red Cross emblem,
and you know it. As for the jeep patrols, well-armed
assistance awaits us only a kilometer or so away.

"You know, it is too bad in a way that I really am
not the woman you thought you knew, Milo, for she
could have been, I think, very happy with you in
America. Because of that, I won't shoot you, although
I know I should . . . unless you try to stop us or come
after us, that is.

"*Doh svedahnyah*, sweet Milo."

At the back of the ambulance, she waved her pistol
at Judy and brusquely said to Hugo, "Get her out of
the ambulance, quickly." Stepping into the back of the
vehicle, she stepped through the cargo compartment
to the front and showed the driver and the medic the
business end of the pistol. "If you two want to be alive

to get demobilized, you'll do exactly as I say for the next few minutes."

Staring wide-eyed at the black hole of the muzzle, the driver gulped once, his prominent Adam's apple bobbing, and said, "Yes *ma'am!* Ah'll sho'ly do enythin' you says."

Buck had been stunned by the blow from Hugo's pistol, but not rendered really unconscious, and a whimper from the semiconscious Judy as Hugo jerked her body out of the ambulance and dropped her to the ground brought the short, wiry man into full awareness.

Standing in the doorway of the headquarters building, neither Milo nor Sergeant Stupsnasig ever could say precisely what happened then. At one moment, Hugo was turning to clamber into the back of the ambulance, and only an eyeblink of time later, he was lying thrashing in the dirt, shrieking dementedly, with blood bubbling up out of his mouth.

Betty appeared at the back doors of the ambulance, took but a single look at Hugo, then absently shot him twice in the forehead before slamming the doors shut.

Buck, blood pouring down from the lacerated side of his head, unnoticed, sat in the dust with Judy cradled in his arms, seemingly unmindful of anything else going on around him, crooning to her softly in French.

As the ambulance driver changed gears, Milo dove out of the doorway, came up with Hugo's dropped pistol and began to rapid-fire offhand at the departing vehicle.

A deep voice spoke just behind him, saying, "Hang on a second, major."

He looked around just in time to see Sergeant Stupsnasig withdraw her hand from the front of her wellstuffed shirt. The hand was holding a Smith&Wesson revolver. The big woman dropped to a squat, took a two-handed grip on the snub-nosed weapon and, with five shots, blew out both of the rear tires of the ambulance.

As the big woman ejected the cases and began to stuff .38 caliber cartridges into the cylinder, the quiet of the post was suddenly broken by the whooping wails of sirens and the roars of jeep engines on the perimeters, almost drowning out the shouts of the guards. From somewhere not too far distant, around some of the twists and turns of the abominably surfaced dirt road leading to the main post, came the unmistakable sound of a .50 caliber machine gun firing short, controlled bursts.

Milo checked the magazine of the Colt Woodsman to find three rounds left, plus the one in the chamber. Cautiously, he began to walk over to where the ambulance had slewed to a halt just beyond the gate to the smaller compound. But before he reached it, the gates of the main compound swung wide to admit a half-track and a three-quarter-ton field car—the former mounting a .50 caliber machine gun and filled with armed troops, the latter mounting a large radio set and conveying General Barstow, who held a Thompson submachine gun and wore a field jacket over his class-A uniform.

Pulling around the half-track, the driver of the field car accelerated to halt, nose to nose, with the ambulance, turned off the engine, then drew another Thompson from a holder welded to the side of the car and, after arming it, stood up and pointed it at the windshield of the ambulance. Only then did Barstow swing down from the car and walk to the ambulance, his own Thompson leveled and ready, his forefinger not quite touching the trigger.

He opened the door and stepped back, saying, "You two soldiers, get out, *now!*"

When the terrorized driver and the medic had rolled out the doors, Barstow stepped back to the rear and, careful to keep his head and body shielded, banged on the nearest door with the muzzle of his weapon. Raising his voice a notch, he said, "Betty? Tatiana? Whatever your name really is, there's no way out now, never was, actually. So you and Hugo had better just come out quietly. Otherwise I'll have to call my other vehicle over here and turn that ambulance into a sieve."

Milo heard the general's words as he approached, and just as he reached the senior officer's side, he heard Betty's reply: "Oh, no, General Barstow, you would not dare to do such a thing, not with these two rocket scientists here with me."

Barstow laughed loudly, to be heard. "If Russian Intelligence is this easy to fool, we should do it more often. Tatiana, Tatiana, the two men in there with you and Hugo are not rocket scientists, they're not even Germans . . . well, at least not anymore, not for some years. Formerly they worked for OSS; now they work for me, so you have no chips with which to bargain. I give you one minute to come out, then I'll call over the half-truck with its heavy machine gun. Come on, Tatiana, I'm counting . . ."

Suddenly, from within, there came the *phuutt-phuutting* of the silenced pistol firing. The vehicle began to rock on its springs; there were several gasps and groans, punctuated by the sounds of flesh hitting flesh, solidly. Then the rear doors burst open and a tangle of three bodies rolled out onto the ground, feet, fists and a gunbutt flailing. Milo dived in and grabbed Betty's wrist, then forcibly wrenched the weapon from her hand and tucked it into his waistband alongside the one that had been dead Hugo's.

But even lacking the pistol, Betty seemed more than a match for the two ersatz Germans. Hizinger was already bleeding heavily from nose and mouth, and a shoe toe driven into his crotch sent him rolling out of the fight, clutching at himself and retching. Gries had finally managed to encircle Betty's throat with his hairy hands, pinning her arms with his knees, but somehow she got her left arm free and smashed the heel of her palm upward against the tip of his nose. With a gurgling, gasping cry, the man slumped to the side and lay unmoving in a limp huddle, blood pouring out to pool under his face.

Barstow feathered the trigger of his Thompson and put three big .45 caliber slugs into the ground some inches from Betty's head. "That's enough, Tatiana. This is the end of the road, for you, on this operation, anyway. You should be shot or hung or, at least, thrown into a federal penitentiary for a helluva long time; but to be realistic, considering the numbers of communists and fellow travelers that Roosevelt allowed to infiltrate the government and, in particular, the Department of State, you'll most likely just be told that you were naughty and shipped back to Russia, which is why we will have a few chats with you before we turn you over to higher authority."

He turned his head and called, "Harrigan, grab a pair of handcuffs and come back here."

In that short moment, Betty looked up at Milo and said, in Russian, "You know, despite everything, I think I really did love you, my love." She closed her mouth, then crunched something between her teeth, and a split second later, her entire body stiffened spasmodically. Her spine arched, higher, higher, until only her shoulders and heels were touching the ground. Unbearable, bestial noises issued from her mouth, then her body slammed back to the hard ground, her breath came out in a long, ragged gasp, and her blue eyes began to glaze over.

Barstow cursed himself, feelingly, for several minutes.

Some hours later, in his office, with a cigar going

well and the whisky poured, he said, "Milo, I'm sorry as hell about putting you through all this just past, but I had no choice, no options, in the matter."

Milo just sat silent and listened. Not the reek of Barstow's strong cigar, not the peat-smoke odor of the whisky could make him stop smelling the odor of bitter almonds that had arisen from Betty's slack mouth when he had lifted her body to place it in the ambulance. In a part of his mind, he still was waiting to awaken from this long, detailed, horrible nightmare.

"Milo, we knew that there were two ringers in the operation, but we had no idea who, only that one was a man and one a woman. They or rather their superiors, must have learned of this assignment of mine before even I knew just why I was being brought back Stateside. I had no inkling that I had been infiltrated until a week or so before I set you up in the small compound.

"Originally, as you must have guessed, the intention had been to house and feed and interview the subjects out here, where we were better set up for it. Then, when I was apprised that a Russky team was in my unit, I decided that it was just too risky to do it all in the preplanned way.

"Now, the only things that were known about the ringers was that they had both been in my München operation—for what purpose we'll never know. It was known that at least one of them had been a sleeper in the United States even before our entry into the war. A full-steam investigation narrowed the list of suspects, here, down to Ned, Hugo, Judy, Buck, Betty and you, Milo. So it was you six I sent to the small compound, along with enough others to make it appear normal, of course. I might've handled it better had I had a bit more time. Maybe then we wouldn't've lost Herr Gries, Ned and Vasili."

"Ned?" asked Milo. "Vasili? They're dead?"

Barstow nodded grimly. "Yes. Hugo apparently shot them both just before he went to meet Tatiana Nikolayev . . . our Betty."

"When did you find out it was Betty?" said Milo dully.

"Just yesterday," replied Barstow. "The soldier who drove our mess steward over to pick up stores has been careless from time to time in making contacts with someone over on that base. When he was given two silenced pistols, he was observed, and immediately he was back on the road headed here, the person who gave him the pistols was picked up by our people and taken away. Fortunately for us, he had a very low pain threshold, so we had most of the scheme before that day was done, but he also had a weak heart and he died on us before we got every jot and tittle out of him.

"We had sent the two men you knew as Herr Hizinger and Herr Gries through in the normal way, along with a real, if nearly useless, Nazi bureaucrat who had been a midlevel paper shuffler with the rocket projects—that is, Herr Faber. Both Hizinger and Gries were born in Germany, and both lived there until the late 1930s, so it was thought that they could give convincing performances as ex-Nazis, and they were schooled and coached at some length about the proper responses to questions thrown at them by the three doctors. They did convince the learned doctors, I presume?"

"Oh, yes," said Milo, his voice tinged with bitterness. "Dr. Smith was jubilant—he assured me that Hizinger and Gries were the greatest thing since sliced bread. So Betty and Hugo meant to kidnap them, eh? How did they expect to get them to Russia, though?"

Barstow steepled his fingers and looked at Milo

through them and the thick cloud of blue-gray cigar smoke. "I would not be at all surprised if there isn't a Russian submarine cruising or lying somewhere just east of Hampton Roads, in Chesapeake Bay or even over in the James River or the York. A group of heavily armed men was to be waiting up the road to eliminate any pursuit, and a large, fast automobile was parked on a shoulder of Route 60, ready to receive Tatiana, Hugo, Hizinger and Gries. They would then have been driven to where a fast boat was moored. And we don't know any more than that, that's when the man we got most of the rest out of died. But we'll get more —four out of the six we ambushed back up the road there were taken alive and are more or less sound.

"That we weren't able to take Hugo or Tatiana alive is a blow, and I can only blame myself for not checking her mouth thoroughly before I turned my back on her for even an instant. I should've known better. She knew we'd break her, one way or the other, before we gave her to anybody else, and she knew she had a lot to hide, so she did her duty, the only thing she could do under the circumstances; she was a good operative, that one."

"How is Judy?" asked Milo. "Betty . . . Tatiana said she'd poisoned her."

Barstow nodded. "She did—she shared with Judy a small box of chocolates that you had supposedly given her last night. Judy, of course, had no slightest reason to suspect anything was amiss and ate two of the things right after her breakfast. Then when she got sick, she was too sick to tell anybody, even Buck. But the doctors over at the base hospital say that she'll be fine in a few days, a week at the outside—they got her in time.

"But back to you, Milo. You're some kind of fine shot to've been able to shoot out both rear tires of a moving vehicle with a strange weapon."

"It wasn't me that did it, sir." Milo shook his head. "I did try, but I either missed or those twenty-twos just couldn't make the grade against those heavy-duty truck tires. It was the WAAC sergeant, Stupsnasig, with a thirty-eight caliber Smith & Wesson she carries inside her brassiere."

Barstow just stared, almost dropping his cigar from between his teeth. "*Brunhild* shot out the tires, you said, with a thirty-eight caliber revolver she carries *where?*"

"She has a stiff linen holster stitched inside her brassiere, she told me, sir. She carries a hammerless round-butt thirty-eight Smith & Wesson Terrier in the holster, apparently, at all times."

"Did she happen to mention why, Milo?" asked Barstow.

"To safeguard her virtue, sir. She has a very low opinion of the motives of men," said Milo.

Barstow chuckled. "Her opinion is probably sound. But she's the last one I'd expect to need a thirty-eight snub to safeguard her body and virtue. God, man, that woman is bigger—and no doubt stronger, too—than half the men in the Army of the United States of America!"

He chuckled again, then added, "Nonetheless, I'm glad as hell that the beefy battleaxe had the gun and the skill to use it so efficiently. She's a staff sergeant, right? Yes, well, I'll bump her up to tech, and I'll put a nice letter in her 201 file, too.

"As for you, Milo—"

"General," Milo interrupted, "in the morning, you'll have on your desk a letter from me resigning my commission. I've fought my first and my last skirmish in this new war of yours. I made it all through one war and I'm just sick and tired of seeing blood, of smelling fear, of watching people I know die. I have a promise to an old friend to fulfill, and I mean to fulfill it . . . if

I can. At any rate, I want to get back to a life that doesn't include shooting men and getting shot at for a living, that's all."

"But good God, man," expostulated Barstow, "you're a Regular, not just some damned homesick draftee. What kind of career do you think there'll be for a fucking infantry officer in civilian life? Or do you intend to be a gentleman farmer, live on the Stiles fortune and raise thoroughbreds, up in Loudon County?"

Milo arose. "Whatever I do, general, it will sure as hell beat watching a young woman die of cyanide under a clear blue sky, and it will beat the hell out of loading her body into an ambulance. I don't give a shit who she really was or what she really was; she loved me and I was beginning to fall in love with her and I'll be a damned long time forgetting her and the fact that it was your new dirty little undeclared war that parted us and killed her. You can admire Tatiana Nikolayev all you wish for being a 'good spy' and suiciding at the right time. But I'll mourn Betty, if you don't mind . . . and even if you do . . . sir."

"Sit back down, Major Moray. That's an order!" Barstow's voice crackled with authority, and instinctively, Milo obeyed.

Then, in a warmer, more conversational tone, Barstow said, "Milo, if you have to blame someone for the woman's demise, you are more than welcome to blame me. I think my shoulders are tough enough to bear that cross, too. So far as this 'new war' is concerned, however, you will continue to be a soldier in this war even as a civilian, because this war is one that will probably last far longer than did the last, more open war.

"Milo, Russian Communism is a devil's brew of politics and something very akin to religion to its ahderents. It bears many of the aspects of a proselytizing Christian religion—Padre recognized that fact early on, and that's where his twisted little mind began to build his fables about the Pope being in a secret compact with Stalin—and now that the Nazis and Fascists are out of the road, it is going to start steam-rollering its way around the world . . . unless we are able to throw up a few roadblocks here and there, that is. And our job is not going to be made any easier by the fact that our current president and his predecessor both are admirers of Josef Stalin and have come to harbor a large number of men who more than just admire that red-handed butcher in some high places in our government.

"It will be up to us to try in every conceivable way to hold back the international Red tide until we can sufficiently inform the American people of the dangers —both foreign and domestic—that confront our nation and persuade them to vote out the elected officials who are soft on Communism, then pressure the new administration into rooting out the Red vipers now nesting in Washington.

"If we succeed in our purpose quickly enough, there will be at least hope for a world at peace and the war just concluded with Japan, Germany and all the rest will have been fought to some purpose, our dead will not have given their lives in vain. But if we are slowed, thwarted for even a few years, there will be one small, bloody war after another, in one small country after another, all fomented by the Communists as they attempt to take over the entire world. If that scenario plays for very long, the only end will be us versus them —the United States of America against the Union of Soviet Socialist Republics—and I cannot be at all certain that we would win such a war, even with our new bomb as a weapon.

"So go to your buddy's widow, Milo. Marry her,

settle down and sire children and breed horses and enjoy your life. Judging by your service record, you've earned such a life if anyone ever has. But, Milo, you might also pray every night that we succeed in all our aims, and quickly, else the world in which your children live may not be a very nice place.

"Don't waste time writing me letters. I'll see to the beginnings of your processing out, never fear."

Chapter V

When all of the senior menfolk of the Guardian People were in their places along each side of the long, ancient table in the conference room of the Southern Shrine, old Mosix, the eldest of the priests, arose and spoke, saying, "Looters have come. The Shrine of the Arcade has been violated, stripped of many of its Holy Things."

There was a concerted groan compounded of outrage and pure horror from the men to whom he spoke. But before any could speak, the old man raised one withered hand.

"Wait. That was the worst, but there is more. The tracks indicate that those who defiled the Shrine of the Arcade were only three men who rode in on horses. But several of the smaller Shrines have also been violated and stripped of many, many of the Holy Things we all were born to protect inviolate. Those who did these other infamies were more numerous and equipped with horse-drawn carts to bear away the Holy Things that they had looted from the Shrines."

"Which Shrines, High Priest?" demanded the man at the other end of the table, Wahrn Mehrdok, the recently reelected captain of the Guardians of the

Shrines of Nohshan, his big, horny farmer's hands clenched at his sides.

"The Shrine of the Deer, the Shrine of the Bull and the Shrine of the Two Snakes. They surely are most truly the demons called looters, for they heavily loaded two carts with Holy Things and they bore other Holy Things away on their horses' backs," replied old Mosix, going on to say, "True, there are not too many Guardians of the prescribed ages—seventeen winters to forty-five winters—to go against these looter demons, but then do they number no more than the tracks did indicate, the score and two Guardians should be quite enough to take them and regain the Holy Things they stole and slay them for their crimes, their blasphemous activities. Verily do the Sacred Scriptures say that the Shrines and the Holy Things that they contain are not to be disturbed by anyone, that any who do so or make to do so are criminals, sinners. These demons have assuredly sinned and the Scriptures also attest that the wages of Sin is Death."

"Just how many are there, High Priest?" asked the captain.

"The tracks showed six or seven, captain, one of them appearing to be either a woman or a young boy. They headed to the northwest after their desecrations. Two and twenty Guardians should be—"

"Twelve or even ten should be enough, High Priest. Are we all to eat next winter, work must still be done in the fields, lest the irrigation ditches silt up on us, and then consider where we'd be."

"But our Sacred Duty—" began the priest.

"Our Sacred Duty first of all requires that we be around to do it, Mosix," the reelected first sergeant of the Guardians, Kahl Rehnee, interrupted him. "And the captain is right about the ditches, you know that good as I do. This just ain't good farming country, never was and never will be, neither. It's either too much water or not enough . . . mostly, not enough. It's plenty now, but when the lake out there comes to go down like it will soon now, the creek will go down too and we'll be back to raising the water out of it a bucket at the time to keep the ditches all running and the crops all growing right.

"Mosix, it all boils down to just what I said and my daddy used to said afore me: thishere country is damn good for growing grass, but it's pisspoor for growing anything else nowadays, no matter what it was like way back when, before the Great Dyings and all; the onliest way to be sure of living year to year without doing the kind of backbreaking, man-killing work we and our daddies and grandfolks have had to do is to stop trying to farm a place that is next thing to impossible to farm and start breeding stock, hunting game and foraging for wild plants that folks can eat and that can grow without being watered and nursed by folks. I knows you don't like to hear it from me just like you didn't like to hear it all from my daddy, but that still don't stop it all from being true."

The captain nodded, and there was a mutter of general agreement around the table, only the older priest and the two younger ones who stood behind his chair not joining in the consensus.

Mosix shook his head. "And have any of you thought just what would soon happen if you did such a folly? Why all too soon, you would have hunted out, foraged out, and the enlarged herds would have grazed out this entire area. Then what would you do?"

This time it was the captain who spoke. "Move on, Mosix, move on to a place where there still was grass and food plants and game, that is what."

"*Blasphemy!*" hissed Mosix from betwixt worn, yellowed teeth. "To think to hear such wicked blasphemy from the lips of the very captain of all the Guardians! I would never have believed such a thing

could have come to pass had I not heard it with my
own two ears! Have you no shame, then? Must you
flaunt the dishonor your mind spawns, Wahrn
Mehrdok, even while the very looters we are here to
keep from the Shrines are at work desecrating and
bearing off cartloads of the Holy Objects that your
honorable forebears did the duty of protecting?"

"Priest," said the captain, "your problem is plain—
you wish us all to be as stubbornly, as stupidly fanatic
as are you. Think you that you are the only living man
who can read the journals of our ancestors, then?
During the time of the Great Dyings, a man—*man*,
mind you, no god—whose title was 'governor' sent our
many-times-greatgrandsires here to prevent riot or
looting in this town and the surrounding lands. There
was a captain and two undercaptains, there was a man
called first sergeant, several others also called sergeant
and forty-seven others called various things, many of
which terms do not seem to mean anything anymore.
The gang of them were called a company and they
belonged to a larger gang called a battalion which
itself belonged to an even larger gang called a
regiment and this largest gang was called the Missouri
National Guard.

"About half of those men sent as Guardians of the
town and lands died in the Great Dyings, as too did
most of the folk hereabouts. A few more of the
Guardians left to seek after their own dear kin, in
other places, and even fewer ever came back, all
telling tales of horror—of miles of countryside and of
whole big towns in which no living man or woman or
little child still lived, of pet dogs and cats and wild
animals gorging on rotting bodies lying all unburied in
any direction a man might look, of the pitiful few who
had lived running and hiding alone and lunatic or
banding together to loot and kill and rape and torture
and mutilate and enslave.

"Those few of a few who came safely back, Priest, helped those who had remained to decide that it were best to stay here, safely away from the lunacy and barbarism and death that stalked the land and slunk through the corpse-clogged streets of the towns, elsewhere in the plague-blighted and desolate state that had been home.

"So our ancestors stayed here and worked the farms. They fought to hold the land and to protect their new friends and newer families from the dog packs and the even more dangerous roving man packs. And the land was good and productive, then; so long as the mechanical things still worked right and water could be brought up from deep, deep beneath the ground and there still were the big bags of powders to put into the fields, the work was light and the yield large enough to support everyone.

"But that Eden, like the original, did not last. Most of the mechanical things did not outlast the first generation. When there was no more of the special liquids that powered the farming devices and the things that made light and the pumps that brought up the water, then the old men of the first generation showed the men of the second how to dig ditches and canals and how to keep them filled from the creek both in high water and in low water, showed them how to ferment dung properly and plow it into the fields to replace the exhausted supplies of powders, showed them how to adapt or alter what they had to make plows and harrows and carts and wagons that could use animal power for draft. They took long, dangerous trips, those old men, to bring back books and things that would teach their sons how to make for themselves the thousand and one small and larger things they would need were they to survive and keep farming.

"Way back then, many of the second generation were of a mind to leave hereabouts and find richer, better-watered land somewhere. But the men of the first generation had come to love the land their hands had worked and their sweat had watered—their journals tell all of this, Priest—and they also still recalled the horrors those few who had returned during the Great Dyings had recounted or seen. We all might have been far better off had everyone moved out then, but the first generation persuaded them all to stay.

"That was when the first words concerning a sacred vow and duty to protect the town from looters were spoken, written and melded with our religion. There is nothing sacred about the town, Priest—just because our ancestors said there was doesn't make it so. It's not the last of its kind and it's far from the biggest; I've seen the ruins of much bigger ones during my travels before I came back here and married, and as we all know well, there's a slightly smaller one a few days' ride south of here from which we get our metals, so we too are looters, strictly speaking. And I have thought right often that it would've been a sight easier to have taken whatall we needed, whenever we needed it, from this town rather than that one."

Most of the men seated along the sides of the long table looked at their elected leader with wide eyes registering shock and near-horror.

"Forsworn blasphemer, beware," hissed old Mosix. "You counsel sacrilege!"

"Bullshit!" snapped the captain, with a hint of rising anger in his voice. "One ruin is not, cannot be any more sacred than another. Can't you fools see the plain truth until your noses are rubbed in it? We all can read—if you don't believe me about all I've said here today, for God's sake, go into the library back yonder and read the old records and journals. I think Mosix here means us all well, but he either can't or won't admit to the pure fact that he is the priest of a religion that is in large part artificial, devised by our ancestors simply as a ruse to keep their sons and grandsons from leaving this marginal farmland to seek a better, easier living elsewhere.

"Because of this manmade religion, generations of Mosix's ilk have made things infinitely more difficult for folks who have been hard enough pressed just to wrest sustenance from our lands, by forcing them to wagon south to get supplies of metals and whatnot when the ruins just lay there, the metals rusting away and other useful things rotting in uselessness, giving lair to only bats and birds and reptiles and beasts.

"I tell you all, read the records and you'll find that each successive generation of these priests has subtly changed this faith we hold just a little more. The first generation took things to help them from the ruins; so too did the second and the third. Where do you think they got most of the special liquids that powered their mechanical things, or many of the mechanical things themselves, or the powders for the fields? Why, from these so-called sacred ruins, that's where.

"Yet now we not only are forbidden to draw metals or aught else from this crumbling town, we are even forbidden to hunt the beasts that inhabit it. Most of us have tracked her are dead certain that that she-bear as has been killing calves and goats is denning up somewhere in the eastern part of the town, and there's at least one big cat in there, too. But despite the losses and always looming danger to our kine and our kids and womenfolks, will Mosix and his crew allow us to go in and root out and kill those predators? You all know the answer to that, don't you? Remember when Mosix forced the hanging of that dim-witted Snodgrass boy because he killed a few squirrels within the town?"

"Enough, captain!" snapped the elder priest. "I believe that what you are saying is that you will refuse to do your sworn and sacred duty. You are saying that you will not wash out the awful sacrileges and defilements perpetrated by these hellish looters in their blood, as your ancient duty demands. Sad, indeed, was the day when a man like you was chosen to be Captain of the Sacred Guardians."

"You hear only that which you want to hear, Mosix," snorted the captain. "I have said no such thing as you aver. What I have said is that we should not stay hereabouts, any of us that work for our living on this overdry, contrary land. So far as regards the men who took things from out of the city, I'll lead half our company out and ambush them, then either kill them or drive them off. But, Priest, I won't be doing it because of duty or honor or the supposedly holy things they took or the supposedly sacred nature of that ruined town or because you stamped your feet and slandered me like some spoiled, petulant child. No, I'll be doing it simply because the fewer strangers near to my home and herds, the better.

"Now, let's get this senseless business over with so that those of us who work for our livings can get back to that work. Oh, and bear this in mind, Mosix: should any sudden and calamitous fire occur in the library where are the records and the ancient books and journals, the first sergeant and I and all the other men will know exactly who is responsible if not actually guilty of the act. I trust that I make my meaning fully understood to you, this time? Well?"

Mosix was so angry that he could not speak. Small white bits of froth had appeared at the corners of his thin lips, and cold fire filled his eyes. He only ground his worn teeth and growled gutturally.

Captain Mehrdok turned to First Sergeant Rehnee. "Kahl, take a couple of the men back there to the library and remove all of the records and journals of the first through the third generations. I don't trust these priests to keep them inviolate any longer . . . or keep them at all, for that matter. If any of Mosix's ilk or toadies get in your way, you'll know what to do, how to deal with them. Take what you bear away back to the armory and put it under lock and key until the other men have all read the necessary parts. When once they and their families all understand the truth about these parasitic priests as you and I now do, know that God Almighty isn't going to strike them all dead if they leave here to find and make themselves a better life, then Mosix and the rest will have no hold upon them."

The morning of the day after their second foray into the ruined town, Milo and Gy rode out with two of the young warriors to hunt and did so, well up to the north of the lake, with some success. Djoolya and the other women of the camp did their foragings, then returned to camp to perform their other chores. Bard Herbuht spent the morning composing a song about the killing of the strange new beast, seated—with his harp on his knee—near the rack on which that same beast's pelt had been stretched; later, he rode down the creek a quarter mile to a wide, shallow pool to try his hand at arrowing fishes, in company with Sami-Klyd Staiklee and that young man's constant companion, Djeri-Earl Gahdfree, who now only limped a little on his healing leg. The remainder of the young men had ridden out to the herd and now were guarding them while the cats hunted for their food.

Back from his own hunt by midafternoon, Milo and the others had but just commenced to flay their kills when Snowbelly limped into camp, bleeding from a perforated hind leg. Gingerly seating himself and commencing to lick at the wound and its peripheries, he beamed to Milo a telepathic explanation of the injury.

"Friend of cats, Chief Milo, southeast of the place you and the other twolegs have been visiting is a place of Dirtmen, as many Dirtmen as a clan. They have cattle and goats, horses, mules and a few donkeys. Their cattle and goats are bigger than those of the clans—all fat and sleek and slow of foot, with hardly any horns worthy of being so called, born prey, too fat to run and no horns to fight with.

"I had but just cut out and killed a fine, delicious calf and was taking a few mouthfuls of it before I bore it away when a pack of Dirtmen came running at me with spears and axes and a kind of a bow fastened across a thick stick. It was the shaft sped by one of those that went completely through my hinder leg like a dollop of pure fire, and when two more of those short arrows struck the earth near to me, I ran."

Then the huge feline added wistfully, mournfully, "But I had to leave that tender, fat, tasty calf behind."

Milo dropped his skinning knife and came over to squat beside the wounded cat and examine his injury. It was a clean and wide and by now well-drained penetration, apparently made by a shaft with a head no wider than itself. Indeed, it looked very much like the wound inflicted by a large-caliber, high-velocity rifle bullet, he reflected. What the cat had seen to be a bow fastened to a thick stick was most likely some form or type of crossbow, a powerful one, too, to drive its shaft clean through a big cat's thick, very muscular leg with so little tearing or laceration of the tissues.

"Please, Uncle Milo," beamed Snowbelly, "wait until this cat is healed before you ride against these Dirtmen. They owe this cat both blood price and suffering price."

"There will be no riding against those Dirtmen, Chief Snowbelly," Milo mindspoke in reply. "Not immediately, anyway, not if they are as numerous as you say."

"But why, Chief Milo?" demanded the cat.

"Because, Chief Snowbelly," Milo patiently explained, "this is not a clan or even a sept, here; we don't number even a full dozen of warriors. No, until Clans Staiklee and Gahdfree arrive in this place, we'll studiously avoid any contact with these Dirtmen—which means that you cats must leave their livestock alone, no matter how tempting and fat they are."

"But when the clans and many warriors are here in this place, *then* we will descend upon the Dirtmen and slay them and burn down their yurts and take their females and cattle?" queried the blood-hungry cat. "Until then, this cat can wait, Chief Milo, but only until then. Vengeance must be exacted."

Milo beamed no more. The cat had gotten what he risked at the hands of the farmers—or Dirtmen, which was what the nomads called any aggregation of settled people—and Milo felt no blood or suffering price should be exacted, but of course he could not say so to the proud, touchy feline.

If it were possible, he thought that it might be best to try to live in peace with these farmers for the two or three years it would take the clans to strip the ruins. Of course, were peace rendered an impossibility, then Chief Snowbelly would get his wish, in spades. It had happened often before, for some of these isolated settlements had bred some very peculiar people, frequently having ethnocentrism and a raging, murderous degree of xenophobia imbibed with the milk of their mothers.

Throughout the centuries he had been living with the people who were now become Horseclansfolk, forming them, guiding them, he had constantly preached peace and harmony with other groups of nomads and with farmers, but had almost always had to practice war against the non-Horseclans people. Because the prairies were too dry for grain and more delicate food crops for so much of the year, all of the agricultural settlements had had to locate themselves hard onto reliable sources of water to keep their irrigation networks flowing; where these sources happened to be rivers or sizable creeks, there had seldom been problems between farmers and roving herders/hunters, but in those other cases wherein the sources of water had been large springs or small lakes, farmers had often thrown up fencing around the water, nomad herds had knocked these down, and all hell had ensued between the two groups, with the victory almost always going to the nomads for many reasons and with those farming peoples not completely extirpated or driven off their lands in extreme disorder being forever after actively hostile toward nomadic herdsmen of any stripe.

Nor had the presence of non-Horseclans nomads helped one bit, he thought. Most of them had been from their very inception little more than horse-mounted, roving gangs of extremely predaceous, lawless, pitiless, grasping types—raiders, killers, rapists, slavers, robbers and thieves, a few even cannibalistic and all of them incredibly savage and sadistic, maiming and torturing their captives for the sheer amusement derived from their sufferings. They had presented a constant menace not only to obtaining or retaining good, peaceful, trading relationships with farmers and traders from the east, but to the Horse-clansfolk themselves, since a clan camp was as likely to be raided as was a farming settlement or a trader caravan.

A few of the less vicious non-Kindred bands had been persuaded in one way or another to be more or less adopted into the Kindred and become Horseclans-folk themselves, with little or no fighting; a few others had decided to do so in the wake of bloody and costly battles; some of the worst of their unsavory ilk had had to be wiped out entirely—warriors and older women killed, younger women taken as wives or concubines along with the herds and other battle booty, young children taken into clan yurts to be reared as honest Horseclansfolk. Now, most of the nomads for thousands of square miles east to west and north to south on prairie and high plains were either of Kindred stock or closely allied to the Kindred. The remaining bands of professional despoilers had been pushed to the far north, the deep south, the deserts, the high mountains or into the more thickly settled regions to the east where their shrift was certain to be short enough when faced with organized, well-armed soldiers of the pocket principalities that squatted along the banks of the Mississippi River.

The largest and most destructive and treacherous of the bands had never yet been severely enough hurt to flee or come over—the Lebonnes in the north, who had briefly ridden with the Horseclans, then turned on them; the Troodohs and the Tchawkuhs, whose stamping grounds lay east and south of the Lebonnes; the Magees and the Hwilkees in southeastern Texas; the infamous Lantz Gang on the high plains; the numerous small packs of bandit raiders which flitted back and forth across the Rio Grande, as much a bane to the two most northerly Mexican kingdoms as to any other folk. Milo knew that someday these all would have to be hunted down and exterminated was there to be any sort of real and lasting peace on the prairie and plains, but he also knew that to put paid to any one of them would require all the available force of one very large clan or else the assemblage of a special war party gathered from several average-sized clans. Such as the latter plan would mean a vote by a five-year Council of Kindred Chiefs and just the right degree of timing, but he hoped to see it accomplished within the next fifty or so years, with luck.

When all of the men and women had been assembled around the skinning racks, Milo said, "Snowbelly has discovered to his pain and sorrow that there is a settlement of Dirtmen to the southeast of the ruins. He killed one of their calves and took an arrow clean through his haunch for it. We must all avoid that part of the country until Clans Staiklee and Gahdfree arrive here, for Snowbelly says that these Dirtmen are rather numerous and, as all know, we are not. Indeed, were it not for the fact that this is where Jesee-Karl was told to bring the clans, I'd move the camp well up north of the lake and put a good bit of distance between us and this particular batch of Dirtmen, especially as there seems to be something very odd about them.

"As numerous and strong as they must be, why in hell haven't they stripped or at least skimmed the cream of artifacts off that ruined town long since? All folks need metals, especially iron, yet the ruins are full of iron and steel just rusting and flaking away, untouched."

Bard Herbuht said, "Well, Uncle Milo, maybe their needs have always been met by the smaller ruins that surround the larger ones."

"That's possible, Herbuht," agreed Milo readily. "But that still fails to answer the question of why they didn't at least take the made goods from that hardware place or the farm-supply place."

Bard Herbuht crinkled up his brows. "But . . . Uncle Milo, I thought to have heard you say that certain amounts *had* been taken from those places."

Milo nodded. "Yes, both of them had been selectively looted, but many, many years ago, more than a hundred years, I'd guestimate from the appearances. However, there was no sign of any human being having been in there recently, say within the last fifty years. One would think that farmers living nearby would at least have gone into that big building and taken the jewelry and those fine, sharp knives, if nothing else. No, there's something very unnatural about this whole business of Dirtmen squatting on or near to the verges of a rich mine of highly usable and valuable artifacts and metals, yet apparently making no slightest use of them, leaving them all just as they probably lay when the last townsman of ancient times died of those terrible plagues that rang the death knell of the world before our own.

"I don't like things I can't understand, things for which there seems to be no rational explanation. These things usually mean sore trouble for somebody, and I don't want that somebody to be any of us; therefore, we're not going back in there until the clans arrive to give us force, should it develop that we need it for whatever reason."

"But, Uncle Milo," protested Little Djahn Staiklee, "the other boys and me, we all had planned to ride into there tomorrow and bring back a whole mess of them squirrels lives in them big old trees, and maybe some more of them little itsy bitsy antelopes, too."

Milo shrugged. "If you want to hunt the fringes of the suburbs, fine. Just don't penetrate into the areas of the wider streets and larger buildings. Okay? And swing wide around the lake, eh? Ride in from due north, and be very, very careful, Little Djahn. Whatever you all do in there, avoid the Dirtmen or any trace of them and do not provoke any violence. If I can, I want to deal with them in peace—after all, there is far more than enough in there for all of us— but if you or one of your brothers is maimed or killed by them, Big Djahn Staiklee will not rest until he has led the warriors down on them with fire and saber and lance and bow and wiped them and their settlement from off the face of the land."

* * *

Captain Wahrn Mehrdok chose a splendid spot for the ambush of the looters. He armed every man with a crossbow and plenty of quarrels, a six-foot spear and a big, stout knife of the sort that was used in the harvesting of corn. He put two men in each chosen position, that one might be loosing while the other was recocking his crossbow and inserting a fresh bolt. He made certain that all of the quarrels mounted metal heads (common hunting quarrels had for long been just fire-hardened wooden dowels whittled and stone-rubbed to a point, then fletched, as a means of conserving metals). Then they all had hunkered down to await the return of the looters.

They had waited all through a long, long day, fighting a constant defensive action against hordes of insects, constantly on edge, awaiting word from their pickets that the trespassers were coming. On the ride back to the armory in the glow of the twilight, Wahrn had had to break up two serious fights between sweaty, weary, bored and disgusted men.

Sitting his restive, dancing horse and savagely shaking one of the last two would-be fighters in each of his powerful hands, he had grated, "Save your god-damn fighting for these strangers we're waiting to kill or you're both going to be a-fighting me. Is that what you want?"

That was not what those two men or any of the others wanted; that was about the last thing any of them wanted, in fact. All were fully aware that their captain could easily break any more average man in his big, hairy-backed hands. Why, hadn't he, and when barely more than a big boy, been seen to break the neck of a stud bull with those same hands?

While they were vainly awaiting the return of the looters, a great, huge cat of a type unknown previously in this region and of which there existed no picture or description in the ancient books in the priests' library slew a calf in the nearer pasture of Djim Dreevuh. Moreover the outsized feline predator had brazenly crouched over the still-jerking calf, tearing at it with long white teeth until one of Djim's sons had holed it with a quarrel from his crossbow.

Those who had seen the creature averred that it was solid-colored, sort of a dun shade above and with a pure-white belly and chest, and to Wahrn's mind that meant yet another threat to their livestock, for he knew from strictly forbidden forays into the ruined town that the other cat therein was a spotted one. It was purest idiocy to allow proven stock killers such as the she-bear and now this new cat to den up nearby and yet not be allowed to go into the ruins and slay them; he knew it and the first sergeant and a few others knew it too. Now, if he and they could only win over enough of the other farmers to their way of thinking, he would have a chance, at least, of facing and backing down that hidebound old bastard Mosix.

"And," he muttered bitterly to himself, "if a bullfrog had wings, he wouldn't bump his ass so much."

After a brief conference with First Sergeant Rehnee, it was decided that that worthy would take the ambush party to a new locale, possibly a little farther north and west of the center of the ruins, on the morrow. It would be Wahrn's job, he being the best and most experienced hunter of the community, to take a smaller party out and try to backtrack the calf-killer.

Mosix's emissary had objected loudly, of course, to his rearrangement, but the slender, soft-handed man was easily routed by Wahrn's half-serious display of bluster, departing the armory as speedily as he could without breaking into a dead run, his fat body jiggling to his accelerated movements, his face white as curds and his ears ringing with the raucous, mocking laughter of the assembled Guardian force.

As upon the past nights, with all the folk of the camp gathered around the central firepit digesting their meal and keeping their hands busy with individual projects of one kind or another—one of the young warriors fletching arrows, two others grinding ancient brass key blanks against rough-grained pebbles to make arrowheads, others honing the cutting edges and points of weapons and tools on finer-grained stones, one tap-tap-tapping one of the big silver rings found in the ruins with a small wooden mallet up a tapered brass dowel to make it large enough to fit over a horn bow ring.

Djoolya, squatting beside Milo and using one of the fine shiny steel needles she had found and some of the brightly colored threads to apply embroidered designs to one of his cloth shirts, spoke aloud, "Love, I want to know what happened after that enemy woman who had been your lover died and your chief gave you his leave to depart his camp. So will you again open your memories to us, this night?"

Across the firepit, Myrah Linsee, her fingers all heavy with the flashiest of the rings, sat embroidering one of her own shirts, not any of her young husband's clothing. She said, "I remember from all that we had out of Uncle Milo's memories last year, on the autumn hunt. I think I know what happened next. I think Uncle Milo wed the widow of his friend, Jethroh, the woman called Mahrteen. Am I right, Uncle Milo? Am I? Am I?"

"Yes, you are, Myrah," he said. "I had sworn to my dying friend that I would take care of his wife and their children, you see, and a man or a woman of honor must always fulfill pledges. Yes, I went to Martine Stiles, wooed her and married her.

"But here, enter into my memories before I talk myself hoarse, needlessly."

Chapter VI

It was not until shortly after he and Martine were married that Milo discovered just how wealthy had been his late buddy Jethro, and then he was stunned, staggered. Certain at first that he had misunderstood, he switched from the English they had been speaking to her native tongue, French.

"*How* much, Martine?"

She shrugged languidly, in a way that seems to be unique to speakers of Romance languages, and replied, "Fifteen millions, my Milo, more or less, of course; the figure is now some five months old. Telephone the accountant in New York, on Monday morning; he can give you the exactness. But that does not include certain small properties Jethro acquired here and there over the years, or this farm, either, for that matter."

"He once told me," said Milo, "that he owns a villa near Nice."

Martine frowned and nodded. "Yes. I have ordered it repaired. It is said to have been damaged severely in the war. There is another, presently being leased profitably, in Switzerland. There is the little house he bought in South Carolina before he went to England,

120

a piece of undeveloped beachfront property in North Carolina, his townhouse in New York City, the estate that was his father's on Long Island, New York, and the home his father and mother used in winter in Miami, Florida. He also inherited his elder brother's homes, one in Connecticut and one in Cuba, the home of his uncle in Bermuda and the home of his sister somewhere in California."

"Those are not included in the fifteen million, eh?" he said dryly. "Then, pray tell me just what *is* included, Martine."

"Let us see if I can to remember." She closed her eyes and began to tick her fingers. "There is the ranch in New Mexico and the one in Montana, of course. Various petrol wells in a number of places are owned wholly or in part. There are mines that produce copper or silver or something of those sorts—one is in Utah, one is in Nevada and one is somewhere in South America, I believe . . . or is it two? I don't recall, Milo.

"There are part ownerships in coal mines, in iron ore mines and in some other ore whose name I cannot think but who is used to make the metal called aluminium, I believe. There are part ownerships in some canneries of fish and other things, but I don't to remember just where they are and . . . oh, yes, one of them is in Argentina, adjacent to the biggest of the ranches of cattle. There is another ranch, almost as big, of sheep, but I cannot think of where.

"If you will but to telephone Monsieurs MacLeish and Birnbaum, they can send you papers that will tell you all these things in greater detail."

Milo did better than that. He packed a bag, drove to the station in Washington and took a train up to New York City, arriving in midafternoon. A taxi driver's suggestion wound him up in the Waldorf-Astoria Hotel. It was nice, but he found the prices of everything to be outrageous. He telephoned ahead, then took another taxicab to the offices of the Stiles estate's accountants.

There he was treated like visiting royalty, effusively greeted by a high-grade flunky and ushered immediately into a conference room already occupied by both senior partners, Fergus MacLeish and Bruno Birnbaum, hot coffee, hot tea and an assortment of fine wines and spirits.

After the greeting and congratulatory formulae were spoken, Milo got down to cases. "Gentlemen, I want to know in detail just what are my wife's holdings relative to the estate of her deceased first husband, Brigadier General Jethro Stiles. Understand, I had known for years that Jethro was personally quite wealthy and came of a very well-to-do family, too, but despite the fact that we were buddies, he never went into his personal financial data with me. And, of course, I never would've thought of asking, buddies or not—that was his business."

"We can . . . and will give you some information, Mr. Moray." MacLeish replied guardedly, adding, "But perhaps you also should talk with the late General Stiles' brokers, attorneys and bankers, as well. In that way, you can be assured of having the . . . ahhh, the totality of the holdings."

"Yes, Mr. Moray," Birnbaum took up. "You see, our firm only deals with taxes and, therefore, only those assets that fall under the scansion of the Department of the Treasury."

"That is," said MacLeish, "domestic incomes, only."

"Just how much is the total worth of the estate, gentlemen? Do you know?" asked Milo bluntly.

MacLeish looked at Birnbaum and Birnbaum looked at MacLeish, then both began to leaf through the stacks of manila folders. At length, MacLeish held a whispered consultation with Birnbaum, then closed the last folder and answered.

"In the neighborhood of twenty-one million dollars, Mr. Moray. But please understand, the figure only represents domestic holdings, and very little of the figure is fluid. Most of it is in land, buildings and equipment, cattle, sheep, horses and such, crops not yet harvested, fishing boats, machinery, that sort of thing."

"Of course," Birnbaum added, "if you and Mrs. Sti—ahhh, Mrs. Moray should be in need of cash just now, it might be wise to speak with the late general's personal attorney to whom he entrusted, I am given to understand, the keys to certain safety-deposit boxes as well as the numbers to certain Swiss accounts."

Milo got the same treatment when he mentioned his name to the receptionist of the law firm and assumed that the accountants must have telephoned ahead of him. Although it was a slightly luxurious office rather than a conference room into which a secretary ushered him and although only a single man awaited him, there still was hot coffee, hot tea and a larger selection of booze than the previous offerings.

"So you're Milo Moray, hey?" said John Bannister, while shaking hands. "Poor Jethro often spoke and wrote about you. God bless you, you were and are the best friend he ever had. Just how and where did he die? Do you know?"

"He died in my arms, Mr. Bannister, shot in the back by a Hitler Youth sniper all of about fourteen years old, on the street of a little town in Germany, at the very tail end of the war, more's the pity," said Milo solemnly. "And only a few minutes before, I had been pooh-poohing his presentiments that he soon would be dead.

"And, by the way, he entrusted to me a large sealed envelope to be delivered to his attorneys on his death, but no name was given and the accountants mentioned that you are not the only law firm he retained."

"No, they were wrong, Mr. Moray. I was Jethro's only attorney. The other firm represented his late father and the estate, which did not come into Jethro's sole ownership until his younger sister died in 1934. After he and I weighed and discussed the matter, it was our mutual decision to allow them to continue to manage the bulk of the estate matter, for, after all, they knew it in depth and had more than adequate personnel. At that time, my own staff was not so large, you see.

"But back to Jethro's presentiment, yes, I saw that several times in my squadron, during the war. I was a Marine Corps fighter pilot. I believe you were an infantry officer. First lieutenant? Or am I wrong?"

Milo nodded. "I was discharged in the rank of major, Mr. Bannister, but, yes, I was an infantry officer . . . and an infantry sergeant, before that, a Regular, like Jethro."

Bannister's pale, thin lips twisted into a wry, lop-sided smile. "Did Jethro ever tell you exactly why he chose to virtually entomb himself in the enlisted ranks of a peacetime army, Mr. Moray?"

"No." Milo shook his head. "Other than to say that that life was his penance for some heinous crime committed long ago, in his youth. He was very close-mouthed when he wanted to be, which was most of the time, about his inherited affairs, that is. Hell, I never even knew that he was married until well after the war had started, when he took me down to Virginia and introduced me to Martine and his kids."

With a single, slow nod, the attorney said, "Very much against the expressed wishes of his father, his mother and his uncle, Jethro Stiles left Dartmouth and sailed to France in 1915 as a driver with an American ambulance company, but once there, he wrangled his way into a French infantry regiment. Martine's father was initially his platoon leader and, later, his company commander; her grandfather was the commanding officer of his division. He was, I am told, quite a good combat soldier for the French, garnering a number of awards for valor. Unlike many Americans who started out fighting for the French or the British in that war, he did not transfer over to the U.S. Army when America entered the war, but remained with his regiment until the Armistice.

"At the age of twenty-one, in 1919, Jethro came back to the United States, his interrupted college courses and his fraternity life. In some ways, the war and his experiences in it as a French infantryman had matured him, but in others he still was no more than he had been when he had left, four years before—a callow undergraduate scion of a wealthy family, born to privilege, and arrogantly irresponsible.

"With his automobile and his expensive, fashionable clothing, with his worldly-wise and free-spending manner, he dazzled and seduced a working-class townie girl.

"He had mastered certain hand-to-hand combat techniques during the war, of course, and also had learned *savate*. When the girl's two elder brothers ambushed him and made to do him bodily injury, he all but killed them. No charges were brought by the authorities, for both of the young men were possessed of long police records for boozing, brawling, petty theft and similar offenses, but the girl's family ordered her to stay away from Jethro.

"She did not, of course, and their affair was carried on until he finally got her pregnant. There was never any consideration of marriage, of course, for she was just too far beneath him, so he persuaded her, made arrangements and drove her clear down to Boston to undergo an abortion. But something went wrong. She hemorrhaged on the way back to Hanover, and she died in a hospital in Manchester.

"In the wake of the autopsy, the authorities at all levels went for Jethro's scalp with a vengeance. Her brothers came after him a second time, and that time he had to kill one of them and he paralyzed the other, although he was shot twice during the fracas.

"With Jethro hospitalized under police guard, his father and his elder brother, Jeremiah, came up to New Hampshire and began to pull in political markers and grease palms right and left. They ended in plunking down a bail bond, in cash, that was a staggering sum for that time and place, took him down to New York until he was more or less recovered of his wounds, then put him aboard a ship bound for Europe. After more monies had changed hands, all of the charges against Jethro were quietly quashed, but he chose to stay in Europe until 1928. When he did come back, he met only once with his father, his uncle and his brother, then he journeyed a thousand or more miles across the country and enlisted in the United States Army."

Milo shook his head. "Jesus, to have heard Jethro tell the little he ever did tell, you'd've thought he'd done some really terrible things. It wasn't—couldn't have been—his fault if some back-alley abortionist fucked up. And as for the other, if a couple of hoods had attacked me with guns, I'd've likely done my utter damnedest to kill or paralyze them, too. Mr. Bannister, I knew Jethro as only a military buddy can know another, and I'm here to tell you that he was a good man, a damned good man—decent, caring for those who depended upon him . . ."

"I know, I know, you don't need to tell me." Bannister held up a palm. "Mr. Moray, Jethro was not only my client, he was my friend, as well. All that you say about him was true, of course, you know it and I know it, but he did not, could not. He brooded on those three deaths—the paralyzed man died a couple of years later—and he could not seem to ever shake the feeling that he bore an ongoing guilt for all of it. He was obsessed, I think.

"But poor Jethro has joined the majority, now. What about the envelope of which you spoke earlier?"

Milo opened the briefcase that Brigadier General Jethro Stiles had been carrying on the day he had died, removed the crushed and crackly envelope and slid it across the desk, wordlessly.

Even armed with a sharp desk knife, getting the thoroughly sealed envelope open took some time. But finally, the thick sheaf of papers was spread out before the attorney. Lifting two smaller, sealed envelopes from among the papers, he held them where Milo could see the faces of them.

"To be opened only by John T. Bannister, Esquire, Attorney-at-law and friend," Milo silently read on each of them.

While he was reading the two enclosures, Bannister frequently glanced up at Milo, and at one point he hissed between his teeth. At last, he laid them down atop the other papers, leaned back in his leather swivel chair and gazed at Milo for a moment before he began to speak.

"Mr. Moray . . . no, I think we'd better start calling each other Milo and John, all things considered. Milo, Jethro was a very old-fashioned gentleman, in many ways; as such, he simply could not believe women to be at all capable of properly handling money, and the way his younger sister terribly mishandled her own inheritance did nothing to change his mind.

"Early in 1945"—he tapped one of the folded letters—"he got together with a JAG type and changed his will; this is an original of that new will—all properly executed and witnessed and signed, and so fully legal and binding. You and Martine were legally married, the marriage has been recorded? Yes. Now, have you as yet instigated proceedings to adopt Jethro's children?"

"Why, no," answered Milo. "Frankly, I'd not thought of it."

Bannister nodded. "Then you'd best start thinking of it, Milo, and getting it done, the sooner the better."

"But why?" demanded Milo. "I can't remember ever having any children. I don't even know what kind of a father I'd make."

"You'll make a better father than no father at all, even I can tell you that. Hell, you'll be the man who's going to be raising them, anyway. So, if you have the game, you might as well have the name, too, is my way of thinking. Besides, you'll stand to have a sight more than that, Milo. You see, according to the terms of this will, when Captain Milo Moray marries Martine Stiles and adopts her children by Brigadier General Jethro Stiles, he then inherits the entire Stiles fortune, outright—cash, accounts, stocks, bonds, securities, land, buildings, vehicles and equipment, animals, furnishings, boats, leases, the whole damned shooting match."

Mind whirling madly, Milo just sat digesting the pronouncement for long minutes. Then he said, "But . . . but what if I'd been killed, too?"

Bannister held up the second folded letter between manicured fingers. "Had that occurred, there were contingency plans, but it did not; you're here and married to the former Mrs. Jethro Stiles. Now, you just adopt Jethro's kids, and, buddy, you're in like Flynn. As for me, I'm already in; another of these documents authorizes me to take over the management of the estate, all of it, until such a time as you become eligible. I guess Jethro surmised that if I made it through the war I'd have staff enough to take on the estate management, and he was right about that.

"You're living on that farm in Virginia, aren't you? Yes. Well, Jethro had a local attorney on the outskirts of Washington to handle local affairs. His name is Dabney Randolph, I believe. I'll have my girl out there jot down everything and I'll give him a call myself later today. He can get the adoptions started . . . if that's what you want to do, of course."

Milo regarded Bannister. "You just assume automatically that I intend to continue to retain you to run things?"

Bannister grinned. "I sure as hell hope that's your intention, Milo. I won't come cheap, but then neither does the firm that has been managing the estate for so long and neither would any other reputable firm you engaged. If one did offer to work for you for peanuts, you'd be wise to retain another firm to keep track of just what the first one was up to. You'll of course get regular statements from me that won't be written in legalese, either. But I can't give you an exact cost until I have time to examine the records of the other firm, talk to the bankers, the brokers, the accountants, the Treasury people, some men in Europe, South America, South Africa, Australia and Canada. Give me thirty days, Milo, then I can give you a figure."

With his two granddaughters snuggled on his lap and his grandson sitting on the arm of the overstuffed chair with his head on one bony shoulder, Etienne Duron looked to be truly at peace with the world that had used him and most of his family and possessions so cruelly in the last decade.

Grief and long privation had prematurely aged the retired army officer to a marked degree, so that he appeared ten to fifteen years older than his actual fifty-three. But despite his emaciation, his patched shirt and his worn-shiny, threadbare suit, he was most distinguished-looking, Milo thought upon his initial introduction by Martine to her widowed father.

Shortly, they sat down to a meal consisting of a boned and poached fish in aspic, a small bowl of beans, a loaf of cheap bread and a bare liter of sour *vin ordinaire*.

With a sad smile, Grandpère Duron apologized, saying, "As one ages, the appetite goes and one forgets to buy food." It was a patently lame excuse and Milo was quick to notice that the older man ate only a bit of bread and drank one glass of the terrible wine.

To little Per's loud plaint of being still hungry when no more food remained upon the table, Milo said, "It's time for you and your sisters to go upstairs with Mathilde and have your nap. When you wake up, there will surely be some chocolates and marzipan waiting for you. Now all of you kiss your mother and go."

While Martine and her father were clearing the table, Milo went out and walked until he found a taxi. The prewar Austin looked to be held together only by rust, friction tape and prayer, but it did get him to one of the addresses given him by John Bannister. A brief conversation and the handing over of a letter of international credit and Milo was again being accorded the by now familiar royal treatment by the fawning bank staff.

He stepped from the bank through the open rear door of a Rolls-Royce, but before he would allow the uniformed chauffeur to start the engine, he explained certain of his needs to the slim, handsome man.

Wide-eyed, amazement tinged with something else in his voice, the driver turned to face Milo, saying, "*You* are the new son-in-law of Colonel Etienne Duron? Please pardon my impertinence, monsieur, but the order was for only one Monsieur Moray. Is monsieur by any chance a former *capitaine* of *infantrie* of the American Army, and is his Christian name Milo?"

Puzzled, Milo just nodded. "Yes, my full name is Milo Moray, and yes, I was a captain of infantry for a while, though I retired in the rank of major. I'm just another civilian now."

The chauffeur stared at him, something approaching awe shining from his dark eyes. Then he turned, started the car, put it into gear and smoothly pulled out into the busy traffic, blithely cutting off a huge, lumbering van with a body of corrugated metal, a battered taxi and a bus in his acceleration across three lanes of fast-moving vehicles.

The man handled the car with flawless perfection, but drove at a breakneck pace and with gut-wrenching abandon, rounding traffic circles with a careless disregard of other vehicles of any size, somehow managing to avoid stationary obstacles when he zipped through right-angle turns into narrow side streets. Every so often, he would come to a full stop, apply the brake and get out with a murmured *"Moment, s'il vous plaît, M'sieu Moray."*

The first stop was to speak with a one-legged bootblack, lead him over to the Rolls and let him look in at Milo. The next one was a gendarme, then there were assorted men and a few women, another gendarme, a score or more of taxi drivers and porters outside the main railway passenger terminal. Finally on their way to the main market, the chauffeur stopped only three times more—two women who looked to Milo like cheap streetwalkers and yet another gendarme.

Bidding M'sieu Moray to remain in the car, the chauffeur sped off afoot into the crowded, bustling open-air market. He was nowhere in sight when, by ones and twos and three, men and women and even

children began to slowly dribble up to finally surround
the Rolls, all of them staring in silence at Milo,
whispering among themselves and pointing. Milo
began to get a little edgy; he was carrying a fair sum of
money now, in cash, and not a few of the crowd
looked the part of hoodlums. He was a little relieved
when a cassocked priest pushed through the crowd and
walked up to the car, then tapped on the rolled-up
window.

Once the glass no longer separated them, the priest
asked, "Is M'sieu then truly the kind and generous
sometime-*capitaine* Milo Moray, he who was so unbe-
lievably kind to a poor man he never did meet and to
that poor man's desperate young daughter?"

"Father," Milo asked his own question, "please, tell
me, just what the devil is going on. From the moment
I got into this car, the driver has been running it all
over Paris and hopping out at odd times and places to
drag people over to look at me as if I were some well-
known dignitary or a two-headed calf."

The priest did not smile, just nodded with sol-
emnity. "You are most well known, m'sieu, but by
name and charitable deeds only. Those who fought les
Boches in Paris and her environs, those of the
Resistance, we all have honored your name for more
than three years, now. After the untimely demise of
the brave Henri Gallion—he never, ever fully recovered from the unmentionable things that the
Gestapo did to him, and despite the warmth and food
and comforts and medicines that your unparalleled
generosity afforded his last few months of life, he died
of pneumonia in July of 1945—his daughter, Nicole,
and a prostitute named Angélique Laroux spreawd
your fame far and wide within the circle of the
Resistance. We tried many times to find you, and we
did find your former battalion and company, only to

discover that you had been seconded to another unit, but when we tried to find that unit, we always struck a blank wall, for some reason. Frankly, after all this time, we had despaired of ever finding you alive.

"Now, to suddenly find that you not only still live and are in Paris and even are married to a Frenchwoman, the daughter of a most distinguished, decorated, retired French army officer, this all your chauffeur, Marcel Noyes, found so exciting that he could not but share with his fellow Resistance friends the rare honor of actually seeing you. I, too, am most honored, M'sieu Moray. I would be the more so could I shake your hand in the American fashion. I am Father Arsenné Mullineaux." The hand extended through the window was a bit grubby, but his clasp was firm.

Upon seeing the handclasp, the people moved in closer, and a big, burly bear of a man pushed forward out of the crowd. As he came in closer, Milo thought that he looked a little like the common conception of a pirate, with his flapping eyepatch, his scar-laced face and his rolling gait. The husky man's bearing marked him as a leader, and the priest instinctively moved a little to the side for him, thus confirming his status.

"It is really him, then, Father Arsenné?" he asked. "Marcel told the whole truth for a change, then, and we at last have found Milo Moray?" His voice matched his size, a basso growl.

Upon being assured that this gentleman in the back seat of the Rolls was the one, only and original *Monsieur le Capitaine* Milo Moray, he said shyly, "M'sieu, this sight of you is the God-sent answer to many a prayer. When you could not be found, after Germany capitulated, it was feared by many that *les Boches* had killed you and that you lay somewhere in an unmarked grave.

"I am René Febvre, called l'Petit. I have done many

bad things in my forty years, but still I would shake the hand of a true saint, if he would permit me . . . ?"

At Milo's acquiescence, the hand that came through the window was at least as large as that of a mountain gorilla and almost as hairy. There was the clear hint of enormous strength in the hand, but also of gentleness.

Before the car at last left the market area, Milo knew that he had shaken at least two hundred hands, and many of the shakers, the women in particular, had also kissed his hand. And when leave they did, the spacious interior of the Rolls was solidly packed with foodstuffs and wine, cognac and cordials. Nor had Milo been allowed to pay a single franc for any of it.

When he had begun to try to stuff bills into the pockets of those who were loading the best of their wares into the car, the hulking Rene Febvre had gently taken his arm and led him back toward the car, rumbling softly, "M'sieu Moray, please do not embarrass these men and women. You did so very much for a man and a girl who are heroes to us of the *Resistance*, your generous gift can never ever be repaid, but please let us try in our own small ways."

They were only a short distance from their destination when Milo suddenly remembered his promise to Per, his adopted son. "Marcel, if there is anyplace left in this car to stow it, I promised to bring my children some *bonbons*, *chocolats* and *pâtés d'amandes*, perhaps. Could we stop at a shop that sells them?"

The chauffeur did not speak a word, just made a U-turn that sent piles of foodstuffs toppling throughout the car's interior, came within bare centimeters of clipping a war-worn GI jeep with the unit markings painted over and a crate of guinea fowl in the back. The jeep driver took a hand off the wheel long enough to shake a clenched fist and shout spluttering curses. At the next turn, the Rolls came within millimeters of taking out a gendarme, but the chauffeur drove serenely on, seeming to not even hear the whistle shrilling angrily behind him.

Completely blocking a short, narrow street, Marcel double-parked before a tiny shop with the legend CONFISERIE painted on its front. Ignoring the bills in Milo's outstretched hand—there being no way that Milo could have easily gotten out of the overstuffed car himself—the black-suited man got out of the vehicle and entered the shop, shortly emerging with a box that looked to hold at least two kilos and followed by an elderly woman and a younger man who both peered in at Milo for the length of time that it took Marcel to get going again.

Close to Etienne Duron's house, Marcel stopped once more to engage two men in conversation, then proceeded the remainder of the distance much more slowly, with the two men standing on the running boards and clinging to the roof pillars while staring at Milo with looks of dumb adoration.

As the chauffeur and his two assistants began the job of unloading the well-loaded car into the kitchen and pantry of the house, Martine took Milo's arm and protested, "*Mon Dieu*, husband, you bought far too much. My father has no refrigeration here, as we have in America, so most of this all will rot before it can be used. And what must have been the cost of all this, this . . . ?"

"Much less than one would think, my dear," said Milo dryly, adding, "In point of pure fact, nothing, not a single franc."

The woman just stared at him. "Milo, have you been drinking, perhaps?"

Marcel, who had overheard the exchange, chose that moment to say, "Madame does not know, then, M'sieu Moray? Of course not, she does not sound to have lived in France for some years, and m'sieu is clearly a man of surpassing modesty, as regards his charity."

Turning to Martine, he said solemnly, "Madame Moray, it is your great honor to be the wife of a very good and most saintly man. For long years we all thought him killed by *les Boches*, mourned his death, made the repose of his compassionate soul the object of thousands of masses, tens of thousands of candles and millions of heartfelt prayers.

"It was I, Marcel Eudes Noyes, who first discovered today that the saintly *Capitaine* Milo Moray still lives. Soon all of Paris will know and rejoice, then all of France."

Colonel Duron had been seated, looking rather stunned as the three grunting, groaning men bore the vast quantities of comestibles and beverages into his house. Overhearing, his head swiveled on his bony, loose-skinned neck. "But of course," he pronounced slowly, "my poor memory is failing me; *that* is why your name sounded so very familiar when first Martine wrote to me of you. To think, I greeted you this day, ate across the same table from you . . . yet, in my fast-encroaching senility, I failed to connect facts."

Martine just looked helplessly from Marcel to Milo to her father. "What in the world are you two babbling about? Tell me, please!"

Duron took his daughter's hand and drew her down on the bench at his side. "Martine, do you have memory of a man named Henri Gallion? No, you probably would not, you were very young when last you might have heard that name. Henri was badly wounded at the Marne in the Great War; nonetheless, he recovered sufficiently to become a most successful businessman, despite all of the economic problems. But because of his wounds, he was not called to fight *les Boches* in 1940, though his son was and that young man died trying to hold a line in Flanders. His wife suffered a seizure when the news reached them and she, too, died shortly thereafter.

"His young daughter, Nicole, left the convent school then, to care for her bereaved father. She stood at his side, then led him home weeping after they had watched the arrogant German army march into Paris. But unlike far too many French men and French women, those two would not let matters so rest, would not lower themselves to passive collaboration with the occupying enemy. They carried on the war in their own quiet ways."

"Henri Gallion sat high in the council of the *Résistance*, Madame Moray," put in Marcel Noyes, "and his brave daughter became a courier, her carefully cultivated appearance of youth, modesty and utter innocence saving her in many times and places as she did her most dangerous work for France."

Duron nodded and continued his recital. "For almost five years, Henri Gallion and Nicole were able to hoodwink *les Boches*, leading an overt life and a covert life simultaneously. Then, only a month or less before the liberation of Paris, both father and daughter were taken away by SS men and Gestapo agents. Poor Gallion himself was savagely tortured, maimed, deliberately crippled."

Martine paled perceptibly as Marcel interjected, "*Les Boches* did not ever know just how big a fish they had netted in Henri Gallion. Had either he or little Nicole broken under the questionings and the mistreatments, I shudder to think what might then have chanced, madame, for me and thousands of other loyal French men and women.

"But neither of them broke. Even when the pigs tore out both of Henri's eyes, drilled through into the quivering nerves of most of his teeth, rammed steel spikes into his fingertips after they already had torn out his nails with pincers. They placed wirings in the

most sensitive portions of his body and ran electrical
currents through them, burning him severely in many
places, they crushed his . . . his masculinities in a small
vise . . . and almost all of this, they forced Nicole to
watch being done.

"But despite the very worst, Henri never divulged
even a hint of his association with *la Résistance*, nor
did Nicole. She was put in prison and there raped
repeatedly; he was placed in a prison hospital to
recover sufficiently to be sent to a concentration camp
in Germany, but before he could be entrained, Paris
was liberated.

"Henri Gallion and Nicole were free, yes, as was our
Paris, but free as well to slowly starve, for what can a
blind jeweler with maimed hands do? Many were the
offers of money and of food and fuel, but Henri
Gallion had his pride intact still, and he well knew
that most or all of those extending help to him were in
only barely better condition themselves, and he would
take nothing, rather having Nicole sell his available
stock, then family pieces to eke out a precarious
existence.

"Madame Moray, when there was nothing left to
sell, Nicole was become frantic, for she never had
learned any sort of trade. Then a woman she had met
in the prison, one Angélique Laroux, a most accomplished courtesan, offered to take Nicole on as an
apprentice and journeyed north with her, into Germany, to answer the gold-edged summons of a high-
ranking American officer.

"But poor Nicole, whose only sexual experiences had
been brutal rapes done upon her in the German
prison, her courage failed her at the sticking point and
she could not force herself to go through with the
arrangement. The man was your husband, Madame
Moray, and when he saw her anguish and terror, he
gave her his bed and slept himself upon the hard floor.

"Later, when he had been told by Angélique of the tribulations of Nicole and her father, he arranged to sell certain of his personal possessions to the high-ranking officer, a Brigadier Estilles, I believe, and give the value—hundreds of thousands of francs, it was—to Nicole for the proper care of her father. Nicole's last sight of that selfless man was of him still asleep in the grayness of the dawn, wrapped in a blanket upon the cold floor.

"Both Nicole and Angélique have many times sworn before God that as *le Capitaine* Moray lay there sleeping, there was a dim, glowing radiance about his face and his head, such as the saints owned. And already, one hears, many of those who this day have been touched by him attest that a good, warm tingling of the power of grace has passed from his hand to them, and one of those so attesting is a priest of God, Father Arsenné.

"Madame, it is very possible that your good husband is truly a saint."

Chapter VII

A little before sundown, Captain Wahrn Mehrdok stalked into the quarters of the priests, saying, "Mosix, chase this passel of parasites out of here or come outside with me. We two need to talk . . . alone, if you please."

The old priest feared Wahrn or any other man who had proved that he could or would stand up to parochial authority, and he was not about to go outside his comfortable home into the darkening countryside with the captain. Grudgingly, therefore, he told the six younger priests and acolytes to leave, but signed them all not to go far.

When the last of the six had shuffled out, Captain Mehrdok took one of the now-vacated seats at the dining table, used his belt knife to take a thick slice from the veal roast, slapped the slab of meat between two slices of pale-brown wheaten bread and took a big bite before beginning to talk.

"Cat-killed or not, this is tasty veal, Mosix. Don't look so damned surprised—we all heard of how you holy-mouthed half that calf carcass out of Djim Dreevuh's wife. I'd advise you to savor this veal fully, because it may well be the last food you get without working for it—physically working, Mosix, not just running your mouth, you and the rest of your crew."

Mosix drew himself up, his eyes shining his wrath. "You lie, Wahrn Mehrdok, for the council would never . . ."

The captain swallowed his mouthful of bread and veal, then grinned. "The entire council has, as of last night, read the significant parts of the old journals, the written records of our fathers and theirs, Mosix, and precious few of them are stupid men, you know it and I know it. So don't expect too very much support to be voted you in council, from now on.

"And another thing. Once we're sure that the men who rode into the so-called shrine-city and out again are gone for good, as they seem to be, since there's no recent traces of them in the ruins, I am going to take a large hunting party into there and root out the she-bear and the two big cats we know of, as well as any other big, dangerous beasts we can find. That much done, we're going to start doing what we should've done donkey's years back—mining the ruins for metals and anything else still usable—whether you like it or not. Is everything clear now, Mosix? You and your sons and nephews have lost your power, your hold over our people."

"*Sacrilege!*" hissed Mosix, in cold rage.

"Cowflop," remarked Wahrn good-naturedly, as he drew his knife and severed another thick chunk of the roasted veal, then dipped himself up a mugful of barley ale from the broached cask. But all things considered, Wahrn Mehrdok was not a brutal or a callous man, and there was a hint of gentleness in his voice as he spoke again, even a bare hint of sympathy for his old enemy, the priest.

"I've been called many things over the years, Mosix, by you and by others, but nobody has ever been able to truthfully call me an insensitive man. It's gonna be hard on you and the younguns, at first, I knows that; none of you has ever put in a decent day's work in all your life, nor your daddy and his, afore you."

Mosix stiffened. "I have labored all of my life in the Vineyards of Our Lord . . . *eeek!*" He squeaked and would have flinched away, had not his right wrist been suddenly pinioned in the iron grasp of the captain's horny left hand.

Laying down his hunk of veal on the scoured boards of the table, Wahrn easily opened Mosix's clenched fist and rubbed the hand for a moment with his greasy fingers.

Grinning and shaking his head, the captain remarked, "Well, what ever kind of work you claim to do or have done, old man, it's not the kind what the rest of us does, for your palm is ever bit as soft as my good wife's bottom. But by this time next year, if you live that long, those hands of yours is gonna be near as tough nor mine."

With his hand back, Mosix regained most of his poise and his cold hauteur, as well. "No matter what you claim as fact, Wahrn Mehrdok, I well know that the Council of the Guardians never will force any of us holy men to labor like common farmers in the fields. We all will just wait until the next council is convened and then . . ."

Wahrn nodded and laughed merrily. Still laughing, he fished a staghorn whistle from out of his pocket and blew a piercing blast on it, then two more shorter ones. "It just so happens, Mosix, that the full council is waiting outside. I had me an idea that you'd want their word on this matter from them, personal, not brought to you by me. Do we convene right here or go over to the Council Chamber?"

The wave of Guardians burst through the door, bearing two priests before them like flotsam on the crest of a breaker. One of the shaken men made to apologize to the eldest priest for the failure to halt the intrusion, but was silenced after only a syllable or two by an impatient wave of Mosix's hand.

When all of the council were packed into the room, standing about the dining table still bedecked with a barely begun meal, Wahrn said, "All right, boys, let's have the vote again, where Mosix can hear it and know it's *our* decision, not just mine alone.

"Are we all in agreement that Mosix and his ilk have battened off the hard labor of us and our daddies long enough? Are we all in agreement that it's high time that they went to work themselves, if they want to eat, that is? Further, are we all in agreement that in the next few years, we means to concentrate on breeding up our herds, hunting wild meat and foraging for wild plants, slowly slacking off on real farming?"

Every Guardian raised his right hand to a chorus of "Yeah," "Damn right, cap'n," and the like.

The first sergeant stated, "It's what our grand-daddies and theirs should oughta have done long years back, 'stead of swallerin' all the swill churned out by Mosix's kin for so long."

"The Lord and His Holy Governor will most assuredly strike you dead for such sacrilegious blasphemies, Kahl Rehnee," Mosix snarled warningly. "Best recant such words now, for the sake of your immortal soul."

"That's your final word on the matter, High Priest?" asked the first sergeant, in mock humility. When the priest stiffly nodded, Kahl laughed and said, "Well, in that case, I'll just take my chances, if you don't mind and . . . even if you do mind. The Lord Jesus we read about in those books you and your daddies kept locked away for so long just don't sound like the kind as would come down on decent mens just on account of them bucking a passel of greedy, lazy, lying priests from off of their backs, nosirreebob, He don't. He sounds for to be a all right kinda feller. Too damn bad you and yourn didn't try to be more like the Lord over the years, Mosix. And as for the 'Holy Governor,' you've done knowed all along and we'alls just found out, it ain't been one since the Great Dyings, no kinda one. You lied to us and to our daddies and theirn about that and about a whole heap of other things, too, damn you, and all just so you could live high on the hog without doing no work. You old louse, you, you should oughta just be grateful we didn't all vote to feed you and your boys to the fuckin' pigs . . . if they'd've et the kinda shit you're made out of."

He and the others would have said more, but their captain raised a hand and cut it off, saying, "You all got the rest of his life and past it to tell Mosix and his varmints what you thinks of him and them, but time's a-wasting, right now. The old sun ain't gonna wait for nothing to come up and start another day, whether you've got you enough sleep or not. What we gotta do here and now is parcel out six grown men and big boys who know less about real work nor a four-year-old kid.

"Here's how we'll do it: I, as captain, will get first pick of 'em. Kahl, as first sergeant, will get second pick. Denee, you and Sam'll get third and fourth pick, then the rest of you can draw straws or roll dice or whatever to see who gets the last two."

"But what about old Mosix, cap'n?" This from someone back in the group of men.

"We don't want to kill him, for all he's done and not done for so long, boys, and to put him into the fields at his age would be killing him as sure as running a sword through him would be, though neither as quick nor as merciful. No, I've thought on it and I think I've got the bestest slot for our esteemed high priest. He can work with Dreevuh's boy at the sluice gates until he gets the hang of the job, then the boy can go back to farming work and Mosix can take over the sluices until the creek drops, then he can operate the bucket hoist. That's the easiest job of real work I can think of, hereabouts."

"Who's gonna feed him and all, cap'n?" asked the first sergeant.

Wahrn shrugged. "He can keep living here, if he wants to, Kahl, for all I care. This place ain't more than a mile from the place he'll be working and he's got at least one jackass, anyway, if he don't wanta walk it. Then, too, he can use his evenings to keep the Council Chamber, over yonder, dusted and clean and all . . . for as long as we keep using it, that is. I've thought for some time now that we should hold council meetings in the armory, then we could use the chamber to store grain in."

The two younger priests could only stand, stunned speechless by all that was being said. Old Mosix had opened his mouth to speak on several occasions, but, sensing the true, pure hostility pervading the room, had wisely held his peace, while his secure and comfortable inherited sinecure crumbled about him. He never had been any kind of real leader, rather had he used the authority to which he had been born, that authority come of religious power over the people; that he had used it despotically, harshly, cruelly, had in part occurred because he wanted for courage, himself, and feared and hated those folks possessed of it. And now, when a few strong words, delivered with power, might at least have ameliorated the situation, he had not the heart to voice them.

The old order changeth, giving way to the new.

Milo fretted and fumed, paced and worried throughout the day, from the very moment that Little Djahn Staiklee and his mounted hunting party disappeared beyond the rolling prairie hillocks until their midafternoon return, laden with a score and a half of big squirrels, a dozen rabbits and three of the rabbit-sized antelope. They brought back, as well, odds and ends of ancient artifacts looted from the ruins of the suburban homes among which they had hunted throughout the day—whatever had taken their individual fancies: a child's telescope, an assortment of stainless-steel flatware, a nesting set of pewter cups, a pitted, verdigrised brass eagle, odd bits of chrome and brass and copper, rusty pliers and hammers and other tools, a hand mirror, a copper saucepan with a brass handle, a bronze poker, two rusted spades and so on.

Upon dumping out the contents of a sack—four decapitated vipers, fifteen gigged but still-living bullfrogs and a brace of big fat carp—Little Djahn said, "Uncle Milo, t'other side of the lake, up north of the ruins . . . well, in them, actually, in the fringes of them . . . it's six, seven boggy ponds, so we didn't go any farther in, there was all the game we could handle right there. And not just game, either, we got another sack with maybe forty pound of roots and all in it— lotus, water willow, water parsnips, bullrushes, water plantains, cattails and I don't know whatall. Hereabouts is rich, rich country, Uncle Milo. I don't think it's been hunted or foraged proper in a coon's age, none of it. Wonder why them Dirtmen, down southeast there, didn't come up and do it?"

"Little Djahn," replied Milo, "there are some small groups of Dirtmen scattered about here and there who own singular beliefs. One such that I remember from some years back held that their god wanted them and everyone else to eat only plants and that those who ate the flesh of any beast deserved instant death; we had to exterminate that group, after they caught a party of our hunters and skinned them alive before killing them. Clan Ohkahnuh, I think that was.

"You see, in the sprawling nation that this land was

before the Great Dyings destroyed it, singular philosophical and religious cults had been proliferating at an accelerated pace for decades. Many of the adherents of these odd groups so detested and feared the general society around them that they deliberately sought out lonely, isolated and all but inaccessible places in which to live, denying access to most outsiders not of their particular bent and discouraging their members from leaving the settlements by various means.

"So, when the Great Dyings did take place—the plagues which did much of the killing being spread by the breath of infected people—more of these rabidly solitary gaggles of fanatics survived than did more normal people living in towns or cities or easily accessible countryside locations. And, of course, superstitious as they mostly were, they and their leaders ascribed their fortuitous continuances of life not to the happenstance of their lack of exposure to carriers of pneumonic plagues but to the efficacy of their particular concepts of life or religion, thus reconfirming their fanaticism in that and all succeeding generations of their kind.

"In those succeeding generations, Little Djahn, a majority of the surviving groups have remained isolated, going so far as to kill or enslave any interlopers who refuse to immediately convert on the spot to the beliefs by which the individual group lives. Most of them are Dirtmen, of course, and some few have died out. On two occasions, I have come across settlements filled with corpses—I have always been certain that one of these had expired one late winter of ergot poisoning in stored grain; what killed off the other, no man will ever know.

"But back to the issue at hand. Until the clans arrive, be very wary while hunting over in that predators' paradise you found. Those Dirtmen, down south there, may well consider those swamps to be sacred grounds, for some obscure reason, and so would deem you to be not only alien interlopers but blasphemers, as well. Actually, as I think on the matter, that same supposition could be of a piece with the lack of recent looting or salvaging of the ruined town here, too. With such a thought in mind, it might be well for us if we commence tonight a regular night guard of the camp as well as the cat guard on the herd."

"Just us warriors?" inquired Staiklee.

Milo shook his head. "No, everyone will have to go at it, Little Djahn—a woman or an older child can do the necessary task as well as could one of us. A sentinel is not expected to fight alone or to fight at all, for that matter, only to awake and alert the rest of us, if need arises. I'll feel a lot better about all this once the clans arrive here to reinforce us."

Far to the west-southwest, clouds of dust arose high into the blue skies over and in the broad wake of mounted riders, carts, a few wagons, men, women and children afoot, herds of horses and mules, cattle and sheep and goats, packs of hunting dogs and a few prairiecats. The Kindred clans of Staiklee and Gahdfree were on the march. This time, however, they were not simply moving half-aimlessly to find fresh graze for the herds and game for the stewpots, but had a definite destination in mind and a desire to reach it as soon as possible, so they pushed each day's march as fast as flesh and blood would bear.

There was, despite appearances to the contrary, a definite order to the aggregation of people, beasts and conveyances. Far ahead of the van, a few mature prairiecats trotted, all their keen senses at full alert for danger of any sort as well as for large game or any meaningful quantities of smaller, keeping always telepathically in touch with van and main body.

Depending upon many factors of terrain and weather and happenstance, the van—those who immediately followed the great cats—rode anywhere from a half to a full mile behind. These were young men and women armed with bows or darts, riatas or bolas or slings, spears or lances strung across their backs, their belts all abristle with the hilts of sheathed knives, a few of them bearing hooded hawks on their padded arms. Although they all joked and joshed in a lighthearted manner, their purposes were deadly grim.

Any frontal attack of the column would hit them first, which was why they all rode in at least partial armor, helmets on their heads and with sabers and targes hung from the horse housings, while axes depended from saddle pommels. But their main purpose was to down any game across which they chanced, for if such offerings were not enough to fill the stewpots of the clans this night, cattle or goats or sheep might have to be slaughtered, and kine were wealth, something that both clans held little enough of, as it was.

But the hunting, thank Sun and Wind, was good, so far, this day.

Younger boys and girls shuttled back and forth between the line of hunters and the main column leading packhorses or pack mules laden with bloody carcasses, their destinations being some open carts, wherein slaves' flashing knives cleaned and flayed and dressed those carcasses, carefully saving every scrap and drop of blood, working always in a thick, metallic-hued, droning cloud of flies. The carts each were trailed closely by a pack of puppies and younger dogs, which licked at any spilled blood and frequently fought briefly over anything dropped through mischance by the laboring slaves.

Mature dogs, well trained and generally obedient,

accompanied the arc of hunters or aided the drovers in handling the herds of cattle, sheep and goats. The horses needed no such canine or human urgings. Most of them were telepathic to at least some degree, and the laggards quickly responded to a sharp nip of the teeth of the king stallion or one of his subordinates. Prairiecat kittens were borne in a cage cart, driven by a human slave of the cat septs.

Behind the arc of hunters, but always within sight of them, rode the blooded warriors of both clans. These men all rode in full armor—most of this being of hardened leather; metal was so scarce and so hideously expensive that it was saved for the fashioning of weapons and tools only, and among the poorer clans even the heads of arrows were often of knapped stone, fire-hardened bone or sharpened horn to conserve metal supplies—their short, recurved, horsemen's bows all strung but cased, weapons and targes slung within quick, easy reach, minds open to receive any communication from the cats or the hunters ahead of them, the flankers to either side or the rearguard who trailed a half-mile behind the tail of the column.

At variable distances behind the warriors came the wagons and carts, wagons drawn by three or four span of brawny oxen, carts by oxen or mules or horses, many of them trailing on tethers milk cows and nanny goats. The herd of sheep and goats were driven on the flanks and fairly close to the carts and wagons, sometimes even among the fringes of them. But the cattle were kept back as much as possible, at least a half-mile back, usually. Where the drovers of the smaller herd animals went mostly afoot, those driving the cattle were all mounted not on hunting horses or warhorses, but on quick-footed, fast, and highly intelligent horses long accustomed to dealing with the big, dangerous, stupid and ever-unpredictable cattle; over the years, more Horseclansmen and Horseclans-women, boys, girls, horses, dogs and slaves had been killed or injured by cattle than by any other single cause—war, accident, hunting, anything.

Dangerous or not, however, the herds were very necessary to the nomadic clans, for no meaningful number of folk could live well or for long through hunting and wild-plant gathering alone. Cattle and sheep and goats were necessary for more than simply their milk and meat. The vast majority of the leather goods of the Horseclans was made of cowhide, the hair of the cattle made felt, horn became many utensils and armor and backing for hornbows, sinew had hundreds of uses, hooves were rendered into jelly and glue, internal organs became liners for skin water carriers and pouches to carry items such as tobacco and other herbs that must be constantly kept from dampness, bones became tools and weapons, fat was rendered into tallow for the lighting of yurts. And because the possession of them was so necessary, the wealth of a clan had come to be reckoned by the number of cattle in its herds. Sheep and goats were important in their own rights to the continued survival and well-being of their owners, but they still were not afforded the same degrees of importance as were the vile-tempered, stubborn, powerful and incipiently deadly cattle, not among the free-roaming clans of nomads of the south, did they chance to be Kindred or no.

Clans Staiklee and Gahdfree had camped and trekked together for long years, and generations of intermarriage had rendered the two practically a single clan, a clan with two chiefs. Big Djahn Staiklee and Djim-Booee Gahdfree complemented each other, Staiklee being a superlative war chief and Gahdfree being equally good at planning the pursuits of peace, diplomatic dealings with those too strong or of too close a degree of Kindred to fight overtly or raid covertly and at bargaining with plains traders.

Staiklee and his father before him had the well-earned reputation of being extremely warlike; within two bare generations they and their clansmen had managed to wipe out or drive off most of the non-Kindred nomads and settlements of Dirtmen from end to end of their accustomed range, leaving only Clans Gahdfree, Ohlsuhn, Morguhn, Reevehrah and a very few other Kindred clans anywhere near. And even these Kindred tried to not stray too close to the stamping grounds of Big Djahn Staiklee for the good and sufficient reason that his nature was incurably acquisitive when it came to cattle and that a good portion of his herd consisted of "previously owned" beasts. The free-roving Horseclans did not engage in the practices of ear-notching or branding their cattle, so theft was a difficult charge to ever prove, and the various chiefs all felt it to be more circumspect to stay out of easy cattle-lifting distance of the otherwise quite amiable Chief Djahn of Staiklee than to risk a bloodfeud over a few steers and heifers and a bull or two.

But despite, and really because of, its wealth in cattle, Clan Staiklee (and, consequently, Clan Gahdfree, as well) was poor in metal. All of the ruins within the range had been long since combed over for metals, and Chief Djahn was most loath to sell or trade cattle for iron. His sire, Sam Hoostuhn Staiklee, had been of equal mind, and therefore most of the metal they did own had been taken in raiding or warring.

Of more recent years, Chief Djahn's most frequent sparring partners had been the minions of Jorge, *El Rey del Norte*, northernmost of the five kings of Mexico. Chief Djahn had never met the man, of course, but he figured him to be a leader much like himself, considering the instant response that occurred whenever the Staiklees and Gahdfrees rode down into his kingdom after cattle, horses, women and loot.

Not that King Jorge's warriors were all that good at warring; of course, few other clans' and peoples' warriors were anywhere nearly as good as those of Clan Staiklee, to Chief Djahn's way of thinking. But the black-eyed *soldados* of King Jorge, though usually well armed and mounted, and frequently possessed of a marked degree of individual courage, were mostly poorly led and invariably did the same things over and over through defeat after bloody defeat, at the capable hands of Chief Djahn and his crafty nomad warriors.

In his way, he was honest, and so Chief Djahn admitted to himself that this sudden move to the northeast was unquestionably a good one; for, of late, King Jorge's *soldados* had come north in increasing numbers, often not even prompted by a Staiklee-Gahdfree raid. The numbers of *soldados* available to King Jorge seemed to be infinite, and although the clansmen always managed to finally defeat or outmaneuver their southern opponents, their numbers were relatively small at the outset and their losses in dead and maimed were adding up faster than young men were coming of an age to replace them.

So it was not simply avarice for wealth and metal-hunger that impelled Chief Djahn and his followers at so fast a pace along the route to the ancient, unlooted town, although he never would have openly admitted it to any other living person, even Chief Djim-Booee Gahdfree.

Far and far to the south, Don Jorge, *El Rey del Norte*, breathed a long sigh of relief and a prayer of thanksgiving when a parched and dusty squadron returned intact to inform him that the barbarians who had for so long menaced the more northerly reaches of his lands had at last departed with their herds and wagons and all else that they owned, headed in a direction that they never before had taken and apparently pausing only for night camps in their trek.

Obviously, the costly war of attrition conceived by the royal personage had succeeded. Now the ranchers and farmers could perhaps move safely northward onto the prairies.

By the time it became necessary to begin raising the water from the shrinking creek in buckets, old Mosix's once-butter-soft hands were become hard and calloused enough to be equal to the tasks required. The old man now lived alone in his home; it was simply too far a walk for the younger sometime-priests to commute between there and the farms upon which they now labored for their sustenance, and so they all dined with the families of their employers and slept in lofts and attics and sheds and stables, leaving Mosix to do for himself, rattling around in the large house adjoining the old Council Chamber and the former library.

The ancient council table and all the chairs had been moved to the ground floor of the armory and the entire contents of the library—shelves, books, tables, everything—to the second floor. The fine, spacious, high-ceilinged chambers thus emptied had almost immediately been filled with bags and baskets of grains—wheat, barley, oats and shelled corn—the beams all festooned with strings of dried squashes, gourds, garlic, peppers, onions and herbs. A brace of young ferrets had been installed to keep out rats and mice, and Mosix had been charged with feeding the beasts.

The old man also was given permission to take limited quantities of whichever grain suited his fancy from the common stores, and one of the farm wives showed him how to quern grain into flour, then make it into dough and bread, but he usually was far too tired to go through so lengthy a process at the end of a day's work, so he most often merely cracked the grain, then boiled it to porridge along with a bit of his steadily shrinking larder of smoked or dried or salted meats.

Twice each week, the deposed priest could ride his ass to the vicinity of the armory and there be allotted fresh meat, generally wild game—squirrel, rabbit, raccoon, wild pig, venison of various sorts, greasy opossum.

Then, of a day, he rode into the cleared area to see one very large and two smaller bearskins stretched on racks before the armory; the two smaller ones were both black, but the larger was of a striking shade of honey-brown.

As he sliced off a couple of pounds of meat from a ham of the fly-crawling larger carcass—both of the smaller having long since become only bare bones— the stripling in charge of apportioning the biweekly flesh willingly told Mosix of the source of so much rich provender.

"It 'uz the cap'n. Him and a bunch of the men trailed back a bear what had kilt a nanny goat out to Fraley's place. Trailed right back into the town, too, she did. They follered and kilt her and both her near-growed cubs. Kilt 'em right smack dab in the town!" The stripling then stood grinning, obviously expecting an angry denunciation of the captain's sacrilegious actions.

But he was disappointed. Mosix only accepted his bloody meat, remounted his ass and began the ride back, kept quiet not by self-control but by absolute shock. True, Wahrn Mehrdok had said that he intended to lead hunters into the Sacred Precincts in pursuit of the two different cats and the bear that had been preying upon stock, but in his heart of hearts, Mosix had never really believed that the man would truly do it. No good would come of such terrible sin, he knew, but no one listened to him anymore, so there was nothing that he could do.

In the new council room on the ground floor of the armory, a dozen Guardians sat ranged about the old, old table, their captain at his accustomed place. They were passing around and scrutinizing an alien something found by the party of hunters that had earlier bagged the three bears. The something was a black-shafted arrow, fletched with what appeared to be owl feathers, nocked with antler horn, wound with very fine sinew and shod with a wickedly barbed, razor-edged, needle-pointed head of bright brass. It had been found in a marshy area just north of the place where the bears had been found and slain, half its length buried at a very shallow angle in the peat.

"This ain't a crossbow bolt," stated the first sergeant, adding, "But it's way too short to be a arrer from a straight bow, lest it was a youngun's bow. And who'd give a youngun arrers with brand-spankin'-new brass heads?"

The captain nodded. "I've seen arrows very much like this one a long time ago, way up north, when I was a hired sword for a caravan of eastern traders. Those were shod with iron or steel, but the heads had similar shape and barbing to this one. Those who carried them and the short, very powerful bows that sped them were mercenaries, like me, all come of different clans of a far-flung confederation of nomads and the finest horsemen I've ever seen, bar none, not to mention their splendid archery and other warlike skills. If a clan of that stripe has drifted down here, we had best make friends with them, and that quickly, too, for such as they could likely butcher the lot of us before breakfast."

He raised a horny hand to quell the rising rumble and said, "Now just hold on, all of you. How many of you have ever fought another man to the death? I have and so has the first sergeant, but we two are all, the rest of you are farmers and hunters, nothing more. Most of you are pretty good with your hunting crossbows and prods, a few of you indicate promise of developing into reasonably fair swordsmen, granted time and intensive practice, but none of those two paltry skills would be enough were you faced with men who had virtually cut their teeth on their swords and axes and lances, had learned the tricky art of loosing a bow accurately from the back of a galloping horse before they'd seen twelve winters.

"Gentlemen, I learned a long time ago that if a man is too strong to be fought with any chance of winning, best to make him your friend, and the sooner the better. Besides, we've been talking for the last few years about eventually leaving here, becoming nomad herdsmen and hunters ourselves. Who better to teach us all the things we'll need to know, eh?

"First Sergeant and I are going to ride out tomorrow and see if we can find the camp of these nomads. Sergeant Djahnstuhn will be in command until we return. Questions?"

Chapter VIII

But finding the nomad camp did not prove to be either quick or easy. Because the alien arrow had been found in the northeastern sector of the ruins, Captain Mehrdok led his companion first to the area north and east of the shrinking lake, vainly, not getting back to the armory until well after moonrise.

At around noon of the second day, at a spot well north of the lake, Mehrdok reined up, saying, "They wouldn't be this far from water, Kahl, so they must be on the west side of the lake, either that or somewhere down along the creek. Let's turn around and go back home today and search the west bank tomorrow."

They had ridden along, retracing their path toward the southeast, for some miles, and the shimmer of the lake was once more in sight when Mehrdok spoke again. Quickly, tensely, in a low tone, he cautioned his companion, "Kahl, listen tight! Keep both your hands on your reins and in full view. Whatever you do, *do not* make any move in the directions of your crossbow, your spear or your knives. There're riders close behind us, on both sides of us and probably in front of us, as well. Don't speed up the pace, either."

First Sergeant Rehnee gulped once, then asked in a half-whisper, "Then what do we do, Wahrn?"

"Nothing except keep riding at a steady clip, Kahl," was the reply. "This is their barn dance, whoever they are—they'll call the steps."

Rehnee could see only a little way into the thick stands of tall grasses through which they were riding and could not imagine how his captain had been able to see farther, but there could be no mistaking the intensity of Mehrdok's voice. Somehow, the man had truly sensed danger . . . deadly danger.

Little Djahn Staiklee and his hunt had once again spent the morning and the early part of the afternoon in the rich hunting and fishing area of the swampy onetime suburbs of the ruined town. On their return to camp, they swung for no particular reason a little to the east of their usual route. It was for that reason that they cut across the clear trail of two shod horses, headed north. Curious and more than a little suspicious of possible designs against the camp on the other side of the lake, Little Djahn had Djim-Bahb Gahdfree, most accomplished tracker of them all, distribute his load of game to two others, then set off on the trail at a fast pace, while the rest of the party followed more slowly.

However, the hunt had only been at it for some half-hour when Djim-Bahb returned at the gallop to report that two riders, clearly Dirtmen, were tracing the trail down from the north. The hunt had but just come through a stand of ten-foot-tall grasses, and Little Djahn led them all back into that stand, placing them well back from the trail and on either side of it, with orders to stay out of sight of the Dirtmen, but to close up behind them once they were within the grasses, then flank and trail them until they came out into the open area beyond, where the young leader sat his horse with drawn bow and his saber loose in its sheath.

Just beyond the higher, thicker grasses, First Sergeant Kahl Rehnee saw a single rider, his smallish horse standing side-on, his bow drawn and its metal-shod arrow pointed squarely at Captain Mehrdok's chest. Spare and a slender build, the horseman wore baggy trousers and shirt of some homespun fabric—the trousers about the hue of unbleached wool, the shirt obviously once dyed a green color but now much faded, the sleeves and much of the torso heavily embroidered in designs depicting animals, weapons, flowers and geometrical designs. Atop his blond head, the rider wore a helmet of boiled leather further armored with strips of horn and antler. His master-fully tooled leather boots were high-heeled and pointed-toed and rose to just below the knee, and to them were laced wide single strips of horn to protect the top of the instep, ankle and shin.

The slim young man appeared to be somewhere between sixteen and twenty years of age, but the cold, hard stare of his blue-green eyes denoted the deadly seriousness of his overall demeanor every bit as much as did the steady bow, the taut bowstring and the glittering tip of the black-shafted arrow.

As Kahl drew nearer, following Mehrdok, he could see that the threatening stranger was dusty, dirty and very sweaty and that his clothing was splashed here and there with what looked to be fresh blood.

Very slowly and with exceeding care, Wahrn Mehrdok raised his right hand to above shoulder level, horny palm outward, in the incredibly ancient symbol of peaceful intentions. Fervently hoping that he recalled the proper way to do it after so many years of not doing it, he mentally beamed, "Greet the Sacred Sun, brother warrior. My brother and I come in peace, our bows unstrung and all arrows cased."

Little Djahn Staiklee started to such an extent that he almost let his thumb slip from off the bowstring. The very last thing he had ever expected was to be mindspoken by a damned Dirtman. To play it safe, he imperceptibly eased up on the tautness of the weapon and lowered the point a bit, beaming in coolish reply, "I am the brother of no Dirtman, no Dirtman of any stripe! How did you learn to mindspeak, anyway? And to do it in words of Horseclansfolk? Do you then reverence Sun and Wind, Dirtman?"

Mehrdok shrugged. "Yes, as much as I reverence anything, brother warrior; for without sun and the rain the wind brings, nothing could grow to feed man or beast. As for my telepathy, I never knew I owned it until I was a bit older than you now are. I was a hired sword with a caravan of wagon traders and became the friend and battle companion of a Horseclansman named Tchahrlee Rohz. He it was awakened my quiescent telepathic abilities and taught me to use them."

"Your sword brother, there," demanded Staiklee, "does he, too, mindspeak?"

Mehrdok shook his head silently, beaming, "No, Kahl Rehnee is a good man, but he has no trace of telepathic talents, nor do the most of the folk among whom I now dwell, though right many of our horses seem to."

"Do we start breaking these two Dirtmen for slaves, or simply kill them, Little Djahn?" beamed Djim-Bahb Gahdfree from his place behind Kahl Rehnee, completely unaware that his leader and one of the strangers had been silently communicating.

"Neither, Djim-Bahb," Staiklee broadbeamed to all, including Wahrn Mehrdok. "The man closest to me, he mindspeaks. I think it best that we take him and the other back to camp. Let Uncle Milo decide what to do with him and the others."

Milo liked the big, solid man from first meeting. Mehrdok was most certainly frightened here in his surroundings of well-armed and cold, if not openly hostile, strangers, but he controlled himself well, polite and calm of demeanor, firm of handclasp and rock-steady of gaze from his wide-set dark-brown eyes.

Wahrn, Kahl Rehnee and Milo were all about of a height, which made them half a head taller than the tallest of the Horseclans warriors and even taller than most of the women. Where all of the Horseclansfolk were flat-muscled, mostly with fine-boned bodies, Milo and the two newcomers were big-boned, with rolling muscles. Of all the nomads, only Gy Linsee bore any resemblance in size and shape to the Dirtmen and Uncle Milo, and even he was a bit shorter and slighter than any of the three.

Nor were the Dirtmen's mounts much akin to the equines of the Horseclans. Not only did the beasts stand a good hand or more higher, they were heavier-bodied, clearly more powerful, with deeper chests, thicker legs and smaller, more graceful heads in proportion to their size. They were mindspeakers; Milo, Gy Linsee and Little Djahn Staiklee had all conversed with them, checking out portions of Wahrn Mehrdok's story. One was a mare, one a gelding, and both were glossy beneath the dust, well fed, and had been carefully shod on all four hooves.

With the evening meal consumed and most of the Horseclansfolk going about chores and various handicrafts by the light of the fire, Milo and Bard Herbuht talked with Wahrn and Kahl, speaking aloud for the benefit of the nonmindspeaker.

"Mr. Mehrdok, you claim to have been a close friend, a sword brother, of a Horseclansman, years agone, somewhere north of here. You say that his name was Tchahrlee Rohz. Was he older than you or younger?"

"Younger," replied Mehrdok. "Younger by about six or seven years. Not much above a mere stripling, truth to tell, but nonetheless a tried and proven and fearsome warrior already, and wise far beyond his years."

Milo nodded slowly, then asked, "What was his most striking physical feature, the thing you first noticed about him?"

Wahrn grinned, his eyes lighting up with old, good memories. "His ears, Mr. Moray. They both stuck out like the handles of a jug, and so big were they that he had to fashion oversized leather flaps for his helmet to afford them protection when blades came out. But big as those ears were, oddly enough, they neither one had hardly any lobe on them. We all laughed at his ears, in a good-natured, comradely way, and he laughed and joked about them as much as any. The two of us, Tchahrlee and me, we . . . well, we were closer than born brothers, closer than any two men who have not been comrades in arms can ever be, I . . . Do you understand any of this, Mr. Moray?"

Milo nodded. "Better than you could imagine, Mr. Mehrdok. I have had friends like that, over the years. But tell me, whatever became of your sword brother? Was he slain?"

"No, sir. After about five years of riding with the train and wintering over in Tradertown with the rest of us, he went back west in search of his folks; he said that he had promised to, and good, old Tchahrlee, he always kept his promises. He wanted me to go back along of him . . . and sometimes, over the years, I've wished to hell I had of. God bless him, I still miss him right often. I wish him well, be he alive or dead. He was the best buddy a man ever had."

Milo smiled warmly. "You will then be happy to know that Tchahrlee Big-ears of Rohz is now a sub-chief of his clan. Herbuht, there, and I wintered with Clans Rohz and Ashuh some six years back. Tchahrlee now has three wives, a pretty young concubine and a

pack of children, not a few of them with duplicates of
his ears.

"Now, Mr. Mehrdok, that I can feel a bit more
trusting of you, just why were you and Mr. Rehnee
seeking out this camp? Wait, don't try to tell me
aloud, open your mind to me, your memories of recent
events. Here, I'll show you how."

Milo drew out a pipe and a bladder of tobacco while
he sifted the contents of Mehrdok's mind. While
stuffing the pipe carefully, he said, nodding, "It's the
same old story, Wahrn. Your people aren't anywhere
nearly the first to experience it, you know.

"Long, long ago, while the technology needed to
bring up water from very deep beneath the ground
and bring in nutrients for the soil from hundreds and
thousands of miles away in vast quantities still existed,
the prairie and its peripheries were rich farming
country; few lands in all this world were more productive of grain crops for both man and beast. But the
so-called Great Dyings—a short, hideous spate of
warfare followed by a few months of uncontrolled
and uncontrollable plagues that almost wiped the
races of mankind off the face of the earth—ended
all of that. Some of the pitifully few survivors of
those plagues continued farming marginal lands for a
few years, even for a few generations . . . until the
machines wore out and the last of the fertilizers were
gone; then they all were faced with the same three
bitter choices—seek out land easier to farm, become
herding-hunting-gathering nomads, or stay and die.
Frankly, I am astounded that you and yours have
lasted as long as you have on that land, Wahrn. Not
many have—generally, it's either the second or the
third generation that has to move on.

"We tried it, you know. The first two generations of
the Horseclans were farmers, settled farmers . . . for a

while, if you can call moving on every ten or twelve years in search of better land a settled existence.

"The place where the first generation grew up and bred was good enough to begin, but then the weather changed to the point where it was just too dry, usually, for consistent yields, so we all moved on north, to the shores of a lake—a far bigger lake than this one, a mountain lake—but there, at that elevation, we found the winters to be so long and harsh that we moved on again. Much farther north, in what seemed at first to be a fine, rich-soiled river valley, we lived and farmed until the second generation were grown and breeding their own families.

"But, once again, the steadily increasing lengths of the winters, the deep, long-lasting snowfalls and the terrible ice-melt floods that heralded each spring all joined to make our position untenable. So, we packed up and moved on once again. That was a very long trek and we were forced to fight our way through parts of it, but we came finally to our destination, only to quickly realize that we could not stay long there, either, not if we expected to live and reproduce. We prepared for that move for years, and by the time we at last undertook the journey, the people were cleanly split into two factions—the larger were become sick of farming, they wanted to continue to move, to become herding, hunting, gathering nomads on the plains and prairie; the smaller faction wanted to continue to try farming, but in a better location than the one we just had left. That larger faction became the ancestors of the Horseclans of today. I've never been able to determine just what ever befell the smaller."

Mehrdok looked puzzled, saying, "Milo, the Great Dyings, they took place close on to two hundred years ago . . . yet you speak as if you were *there*, from the very beginning of the clans."

Milo stared into the farmer's eyes over the bowl of the pipe. "I was, Wahrn. I'm well over two centuries old."

"Impossible!" yelped Mehrdok. "Man, you're a raving lunatic, must be. Look at you, yes, you've got a bit of silver hair, but you can't be more than three, four, maybe five years older than me, if that! I've heard some tall tales in my time, but that one takes the cake. You don't really expect me to believe such a yarn, do you?"

Milo just nodded, mindspeaking now. "Yes, it's a hard thing to believe, Wahrn. Nonetheless, it's true. There's only one way to prove it to you, though. Here, enter into my memories as I entered into yours, earlier."

Aloud, he said, "This may take some time. Herbuht, you and Gy entertain Mr. Rehnee for a while, eh?"

Slowly, inexorably, Clans Staiklee and Gahdfree marched northeastward, guided by young Djessee-Kahl Staiklee, following the same route that Milo's party had earlier traveled. Of course, the clans could not hope to move as fast, cover as much distance in a day's trek, as had Milo's party, which had not been burdened with herds of cattle, sheep and goats. But the hunting had continued excellent, day after day, the only cattle butchered had been those few unadvoidably hurt too seriously to keep up with the herd, and Big Djahn Staiklee had consequently remained happy.

Sergeant Daiv Djahnstuhn, however, was far from happy. It now had been almost six days since hide or hair had been seen of the captain and the first sergeant of the Guardians, not even one of the horses had wandered back to its stableyard. Everyone was talking of it, of course, which meant that old Mosix had heard of the disappearances, too. Daiv expected any moment to be faced with an attempt of the onetime priest—who still had, for some reason, a little power among a few of the womenfolk—to blame the too-long absences upon the wrath of God and the Governor, then try to regain his former status. And Daiv—his wife being one of those who still reverenced Mosix — was not at all certain that he would be able to hold the Guardians steady enough to quell a religious mutiny, especially not with his goodwife, Rebah, as one of the mutineers. Sergeant Daiv Djahnstuhn longed and yearned for the sight of Captain Mehrdok, or even First Sergeant Rehnee, riding into the open space fronting the armory.

Despite his heavy load of doubts, however, Daiv did his assigned lieutenant's duties to the best of his abilities. Turning the work of his farm over to his wife and children, he spent much of his time at the armory, trying to at least look busy, sending out the pot hunters each morning, helping to skin and butcher their kills each afternoon, then supervising the apportionment of game flesh to representatives of the families.

Each night, after suppertime, Guardians would ride or walk to the armory to inquire of word concerning Mehrdok and Rehnee, then to sit, sip homebrewed beer and speculate on just what might have happened to the captain and the first sergeant, whether or not a full-scale search should be mounted for the two, when it should be mounted, what direction should first be covered, how many men should go, who should command said search, since Daiv's job was to stay and command the armory.

Daiv always listened to them, answered questions as best he could and drank down his fair share of the beer (which had all been seized—"commandeered," Captain Mehrdok had called it—from the cellars of the priests' house and trundled back to the armory cellar on the same day that the library and conference table had been borne away), but at the same time he knew good and well that no search would ever actually take place, for something was always more important: crops to weed or muck or tend, livestock problems, petty disputes to be resolved, human and animal illnesses and minor injuries, always something. To get a search started, a real leader was needed, and Daiv Djahnstuhn knew in his heart of hearts that he was no such thing.

But he waited, listened, drank beer and tried to look as if he was doing his temporary job, to feel as if he was taking the place of the absent captain, always knowing that he was doing no such thing, feeling himself incapable of being a real leader, but afraid to show just how far he was beyond his depth.

Then, on the seventh morning since the second departure of Mehrdok and Rehnee, big, beefy Djeen Nohbuhl brought a lathered riding horse to a rearing halt before the armory, jumped off the beast and stalked purposefully toward the door, shouting ahead of himself.

"Who the hell's gonna be the next one for to disappear, Daiv? You? Where in tarnation is that old goat Mosix, anyhow? It ain't no drop of water in none of the ditches. I just come by the creek from my place and it don't look like one damn bucket's been raised since at least yestiddy. You s'pose to be taking the cap'n's place, man! What you gonna do 'bout it, huh?"

The redfaced farmer shut up long enough to apply his mouth to the full mug of beer Daiv shoved at him, and while the newcomer was noisily drinking the cool liquid, Djahnstuhn asked, "Did you ride by his place, Djeen? Maybe the old bastard's sick. I know he didn't come to get no meat last time, but we run out anyway, you know, so I just didn't pay him not coming no mind, really.

"I tell you, Djeen, you stay here and have you another quart of beer, see, and I'll take your mare and ride over to Mosix's. If he's sick or hurt of somethin', ought to be somebody got to look after him and somebody else got to work down at the creek till Mosix can do it again, too."

Nohbuhl, whose fondness for beer was well known, needed no further urging. Long before Daiv had walked across to the panting mare, he heard the wail of the trapdoor's squeaky hinges and he knew that he dare not take long about this affair, or Djeen would be too drunk to mount and ride back to his farm.

Daiv was not a cruel man, however, and despite his urgency, he kept the nearly spent mare to a slow walk the length of the journey. Long before he reached the complex of ancient brick-and-concrete buildings, he could hear the loud braying of Mosix's ass gelding and, as he neared, the blattings of the old man's two milk goats.

The reason for the animal's complaints were apparent when he had dismounted and sought them out. Shaking his head in disgust at such mistreatment of livestock, he led the ass out of the stinking, dung-littered stall, opened the gate of the small paddock and urged the ass into it. Next, he drew enough buckets of water up from the well to fill the trough and forked a goodly amount of hay over the fence to the hungry, thirsty ass. More hay went into the goat pen and several more buckets of well water into the smaller trough, but he knew that this would not be enough to assuage the discomforts of the two big nannies. Their udders were hugely distended, both needed to be milked, but there was no milking pan to be seen and Daiv's inborn frugality could not countenance wastage of the goat milk, not under any circumstances.

Observing the proprieties, Daiv walked around to the front of the dwelling and, after scraping his soles on the edge of a slab of wood placed there for the purpose, mounted to the low, roofed stoop. As he approached the front door, a large brownish tomcat jumped from off a railing and, uttering contrabasso purrs, began to rub against his leg, looking up at him from a scar-seamed face.

But there was no answer to his repeated knockings, and the door was immovable, locked *and* barred, from the feel of it. So, now trailed by the tomcat, he walked back around to the door closest to the stableyard. That one, too, was locked, however, and the windows were all tightly shuttered. For a moment, Daiv could only stand and swear in frustration.

Then, suddenly, he snapped his calloused fingers, smiled and set off around the complex to the high, wide, two-valved door which led into the sometime council chamber and library. Opening one of the doors, then the other for light, he wormed his way between the high stacks of sacked grain to the other end of the long, lofty room. As he reached the interior door that was his objective, he noted a ferret crouching beside a bare wooden platter. The half-tame creature stared at him briefly with beady eyes, then scuttled back among the stacks of grain sacks.

The door let into a short corridor at the end of which was another door. Immediately Daiv opened that second door, his nose told him exactly what he was going to find within the priests' house. There was no mistaking the stink of overripe flesh.

The body, swollen and hideously discolored with rampant corruption, lay on the floor between the dining table and the hearth. Gagging at the close, fetid stench that filled the room, Daiv afforded the corpse of the onetime high priest but the briefest of glances before striding to the front door, unbarring and unlocking it, then flinging it wide open, followed by both windows.

From the place it had resumed upon the front stoop, the brown tomcat strolled into the room and, after sniffing cursorily at the body of its deceased servant, hopped up onto the dining table and began to nibble at a half-emptied bowl of hard, stale, crusted porridge, heedless of the skittering roaches whose feastings he had disturbed.

Hating to do it, Daiv put Nohbuhl's mare to a stiff trot all the way back to the armory, thinking that he would have to send the man to the closest farm to the armory—the Gibsuhn place—to fetch back some men and boys to get Mosix underground as soon as possible; the shape the days-old cadaver was in now, Daiv would not have even considered having the women wash it and clothe it properly; the thing would likely burst or come to pieces under their ministrations anyway.

But by the time he reached the armory, Djeen Nohbuhl was roaring drunk, swilling down a mixture of winter cider and beer, all the while bellowing out what he probably thought was a song and beating time on a tabletop with the work-hardened palm of one broad hand.

Poor Daiv did not know what to do. Were he to try using Djeen's mare again today, he would run a severe risk of foundering her. Then, announcing their arrival with exuberant whoops, the hunt came riding in, their pack animals heavy-laden with two big stags and what looked to be at least twenty rabbits.

The hunters were proud of themselves and had every right to be so, and Daiv was quick to afford their prizes at least a brief examination accompanied with words of praise, before getting down to business.

"Herb, old Mosix has done died, two, mebbe, three days ago in his house. Won't be no proper fun'ral, 'cause he's rotten, stinking, in there. You ride out to Gibsuhn's and tell him I said to bring along his two biggest boys and a pickaxe and a couple of shovels, too. Tell him he'll get Mosix's ass for the trouble, but that them two goats is already spoke for.

"Sam, you and your brother get to skinning and butchering, hear? Gabe, you ride out to Nohbuhl's place and tell his wife she better send in a wagon for old Djeen in there—his mare is plumb spent and he's too drunk to get on her anyhow."

Sam Cassidy dismounted, hitched his horse and walked back to begin offloading the kills from the pack animals, but his brother, Shawn, sat his horse in silence for a moment before speaking to Daiv.

"With just only the two of us, me 'n' Sam, doing it all, it's bound to take us till dark or after, and I got reasons I gotta git back to our place sooner'n that," he stated.

Daiv felt his anger rising, but he held it in check for the nonce, asking, "Shawn, if Captain Mehrdok had done told you what I just done told you, would you've told him what you just done told me?"

Shawn squirmed in his saddle and would not meet Daiv's stare. "Well . . . but you ain't the captain, neither."

"No," Daiv agreed readily, "I ain't the captain, not even the first sergeant, but I am a sergeant, which is more rank than you or your brother got, and I'm the man—Sergeant Daiv Djahnstuhn—that *our* captain said was to run things here till he and First Sergeant Rehnee got back. You heared that, we all of us did. Right?"

Shawn squirmed even more, while his brother and the other two hunters, though clearly listening and watching, were just as clearly keeping out of the matter, waiting to see what happened.

"But . . . but, gee, Daiv . . . uhh, sarge," the younger Cassidy brother finally half-whined, "I got me a dang good reason for to need to get back home early, see?"

Carefully controlling himself, Daiv strode over to the side of the young man's mount, reached up and took a firm grip of his belt with one hand, while he showed him the other clenched into a fist.

"And you got you a even better reason to do like I tell you, boy! You git off that horse and git to work on them carcasses or I'll drag you down and purely beat the shit out of you! Hear me?"

Turning, Daiv then strode into the armory, where he found Djeen Nohbuhl lying on his back on the floor, snoring thunderously in a pool of urine. Taking the big man's shoulders, Daiv dragged him out onto the stoop, careful to lay the drunk on his belly so he would not strangle when he vomited, which he always eventually did after a drinking bout. Looking, without giving the appearance of so doing, he noted that Herb and Gabe were nowhere in sight, although there was a small cloud of dust up the road, while both Sam and Shawn Cassidy were manhandling one of the stags toward the skinning rack.

"Well, I'll be dee-double-damned!" he muttered to himself as he fetched in a mop to clean up the mess on the armory floor. "Cap'n Mehrdok, he was right. It worked! I done just like he told me, and, by God, it worked. I might git the hang of all of this yet." Then he thought and could not repress a shudder. "And I damn well better, and quick, too; 'cause if the cap'n and the first sergeant don't never come back and with old Mosix dead and rotting, that means I'm gonna be it . . . leastways, till we gits around to having another election, that is."

Their funerary chores accomplished, Wally Gibsuhn and his sons reined up their wagon, to the tailboard of which the late Mosix's roan ass was now hitched, before the armory in the early twilight. From the stoop, Daiv could see that a full bale of hay, some odds and ends of ass harness, a half sack of grain and a large iron skillet had joined the spades and pick in the back of the wagon and knew that there were probably smaller items he could not see in the conveyance and in the pockets of the man and his two sons. But he figured that that had been a messy job they had done over there and that since none of the high priest's effects would do him any good anymore, the Gibsuhns might as well have what they wanted of them, just so long as they left the two goats he meant to have driven out to his own farm tomorrow, and maybe that big rangy brown tomcat, as well. The beast had had the appearance of a good ratter.

He waved his arm and said loudly, "Wally, come on in and have some beer with me, huh?"

The short, balding farmer handed the reins to the boy who sat on the seat beside him. "You boys drive on home, straight home, hear me? I'll ride the new ass back, later. And when I gits back, the team had better be unhitched and took care of proper, the wagon unloaded and in the shed, the harness all cleaned and hung up where it belongs and the tools all cleaned and put up. You make your brothers help you out, won't none of it take too long, so don't go looking at me out'n them sad, put-on eyes, hear? Give that skillet to your maw, tell her the sarge has me at the armory and I'll be home just as soon as I can."

As the wagon rumbled off at a good clip behind its sturdy, well-matched team of horses, Gibsuhn looped the ass's halter to the hitchpost and climbed the steps onto the stoop. "Huh!" he grunted, on noticing the big body on the boards to one side of the stoop. "Old Djeen's been at it again, looks like. Why cain't he be happy unless he gets sloppy, pissy, falling-down drunk, I wonder?"

Daiv shrugged as he led the way into the lamp-lit armory. "He's jest like that, Wally. But if you think back on it, his paw was too, so I guess he come by it natcherl."

When the two men were seated at one of the long board tables with mugs of the cool beer that Wally had fetched up from the cellar, Daiv said, "Wally, that was a plumb nasty job I give you and your boys to do, and I thank you for doing it so quick on such short notice. You really earned that there ass, but he looks like a good young'un with a lot of years of work in him."

Basically honest Wally Gibsuhn choked a little on his beer, then said, his gaze fixed to a spot on the floor, "Well . . . actually, Daiv . . . uhhh . . . the ass, he won't all we . . . I . . . took, see."

Daiv chuckled good-naturedly and patted the short man's thick, hard-muscled arm. "Don't worry none, Wally. I saw the hay and feed grain and harness and all in your wagon; Mosix had all that stuff for the ass, so if you're getting the ass itself, you might as well take his fixin's too."

Still looking at the floor, the farmer muttered, "But . . . that won't all, Daiv. I took a big ol' iron frying pan out'n the kitchen of the priest's house and a real steel cleaver and some them thick metal pans what don't never rust and a axe and three flitches of bacon and . . ."

Laughing heartily, Daiv quickly reassured the guilt-ridden man. "Now, Wally, I done told you, don't worry none. You didn't really *steal* nothin', like you seem to think you done. Old Mosix, he's dead now, you oughta know that better'n anybody, by now, so he sure-Lord ain't gonna ever have no more use for nothing he owned alive.

"Me, I got dibs on them two goats, and like as not, when my boys goes over there to fetch 'em home, they'll pick up a thing or two, too, just like you and yours done, this night.

"Now, here, let's have us another mug of beer, huh?"

Before Wally left on his newly acquired ass, Kathleen Nohbuhl and one of her hands drove a wagon along the darkening road to the armory. With hardly a word to Daiv, Wally and the Cassidys, they dragged the sodden bulk of Djeen Nohbuhl off the stoop and tumbled it over the side of the wagon, then remounted and drove off, the mare hitched on behind and her saddle tossed carelessly atop her snoring owner. Daiv was no longer worried about the misused mare, for while the Cassidys had gone about their work that afternoon, he had patiently walked and cared for her, cooling her slowly, gradually, treating her as tenderly as if she had been his own.

Chapter IX

While they skinned a young bison and dressed the carcass for easy packing back to camp, Milo and Wahrn Mehrdok mindspoke one to the other.

"Irrigation problems or none, Wahrn," beamed Milo, "not anywhere near all of your people are going to want to wander off to lead the lives of nomad herders . . . not after they find out just how brutal such a life often is, anyway. Your womenfolk, in particular, are mostly going to prefer the known hardships to those as yet unknown, that's just the nature of females, you can't fight it.

"And becoming nomads is not a thing you can do overnight, anyhow. I'm informed that your cattle, for instance, are fat, short-legged, short-horned beasts of a sort that would not survive even a single season, having been bred to be too slow to outrun predators and too clumsy and near-hornless to fight them. You folks are going to have to start breeding them for more horn, more leg, more muscle and less fat; better yet, start interbreeding them with Horseclans cattle— they're not at all pretty and they produce rather small quantities of milk, compared to yours, while their beef is usually tough and stringy, but they do survive, Wahrn, they survive heat, cold, dust, flies, floods, droughts and predators of every size, and they do it all on grasses, weeds, wild grain and herbs.

"In that regard, at least, you're in luck, for one of the two clans that is headed this way boasts the largest herd of cattle of any Horseclan of which I know. I feel certain that Big Djahn, chief of Clan Staiklee, would be delighted to allow your herds to mingle freely with his . . . but be certain to permanently mark your cattle, for he occasionally forgets just which cattle are his and which the property of others. Indeed, it is often remarked among the more southerly-roaming clans that a fair proportion of his herd are 'previously owned' cattle.

"But cattle are his only weakness, Wahrn. In all other respects, he is a fine, brave and very honorable man, a chief of note, a war leader of rare talents. Are you to become a Horseclans chief, you might do far worse than to emulate such a man, in all ways save his one, very personal weakness, of course."

Then Mehrdok asked, "Milo, why did it have to be destroyed, that pleasant, easy world that preceded our own? Why did those uncountable numbers of people have to die so suddenly and so miserably? Can you, with all your long years of life, tell me why?"

"To begin, Wahrn, that now-ancient world was not all of it as easy and pleasant as you have surmised. The great nation that once covered a fair proportion of this continent was perhaps one of the most blessed and prosperous of all that had ever existed, anywhere, but even within it there existed folk who lived hard, meaningless, hand-to-mouth lives, as had their parents before them and as would their children after. Also, during the century preceding the demise of that world, there was never a time when at least one war was not being waged somewhere, in some nation, for some reason or none; for then, as now, the races of mankind were aggressive, predatory and rapacious, and too, in that time and world, there was the problem of too many people and not enough arable land on which to grow food for them all.

"Added to the coveting of other people's lands was the insatiable desire to dominate all folk, everywhere, which was the driving force of those peoples who called themselves by such names as Communists, Socialists, Fascists, Nazis and the like. These people not only practiced open aggression against other peoples, they also often fomented the lunatic activities of terrorists and revolutionaries in large and small nations all over the world, in the hope that the nations so afflicted would become sufficiently weakened to fall to their arms and armies or to the internal subversion of their hordes of agents within the very governments of target nations.

"All over that old world, Wahrn, folk were leaving the land to crowd in their millions into cities—towns that were miles long and wide—all completely dependent on food, water, fuel and all else being brought from far away and therefore all living within a week or less of starvation and want. In good times, that precarious balance could usually be maintained, but in times of widespread natural disasters, rioting and other civil disorders such as the planned disorders called 'strikes,' the chain of supply was sundered and people suffered terribly until it was repaired.

"You see, it was not the so-called war that extirpated that old world and nearly exterminated all of the races of mankind, but rather the side effects of that hostile exchange, Wahrn. Yes, a very few of the incredibly destructive missiles hurled at the nation that once was here did strike and either destroy their targets or render them uninhabitable for long periods of time. However, the vast majority of those weapons were destroyed in flight, high, high up in the sky, by defenses designed and emplaced for that sole purpose. Yes, tens of millions died in various nations around that world, but earlier wars had been as or almost as costly, and hundreds of millions survived the immediate effects of the missiles, so the world might have picked up the pieces and gone on—an earlier world would have done just that, a world that did not have so many of its people jammed cheek by jowl in unhealthy cities and frightfully vulnerable to contagion, starvation, and the panic bred of unreasoning terror.

"There were those, then, who thought that the plagues were a result of some form of chemical warfare, and some of them may well have been just that. Who, now, will ever know the truth of the matter? But I have always been of the opinion that they were simply new mutations of older plagues, for they moved around the vast expanses of that old world with almost unbelievable rapidity, took hold and slaughtered in areas that had not been attacked by anyone, that still were well fed, living in peace and order.

"The selectivity of those plagues was very puzzling, though, Wahrn. Races that were completely wiped out in some parts of the world were the sole survivors in others. In a few places, women and children and old people were the first to die, the adult men not succumbing until months later, while other scattered localities suffered just the reverse.

"Those plagues did their fair share and more of killing of prideful mankind, but they were not the only killers then stalking about; no, starvation took terrible toll, and other more mundane diseases and injuries cost innumerable lives due to a dearth of medicines and those trained in the use of them. Others died in flareups of warfare that went on as long as there were enough fighters to field and weapons with which to arm them. And even after the national or ethnic armies were become a thing of the dead past, packs of well-armed scavengers made life exceedingly miserable for those survivors they did not kill outright, when they had done robbing and raping them. So long as any sort of order, of governmental authority, existed, attempts were made to keep these packs of scavengers and looters away from as many places as possible with such few police and military personnel as remained; I would surmise that your ancestors were just such a force, sent here to protect the people then living here from the roving gangs of spoilers.

"I ran into just such a group, a unit of the California State Guard, on just such a mission, early on in the death of the old world. Not knowing just who I was or what I was about and assuming the worst, they shot me and left me for dead . . . which is just what any normal man would have soon been. I've never faulted them for it—they were trying to follow their orders, to do a hard, in the end an impossible, job the best they knew how to do it, and after sixty days of living off the land in the Sierra, I'm certain that I looked as wild and as woolly as anyone they had come across up until then. I played the part of a good corpse until that unit had moved on out of sight, then went on about my business.

"A few days after that incident, I lucked across an isolated, very affluent home hidden away in a small canyon in the foothills. None of the people who had lived there had been dead long, and I dragged their bodies out and buried them, then moved in. That dead family had apparently believed in preparing for any eventuality and had clearly been sufficiently affluent to prepare thoroughly, in depth.

"The home was far larger than it looked, more comfortable and richly appointed inside than the outside would lead anyone to believe. Behind the house itself was an underground garage housing three all-terrain vehicles, a well-equipped shop facility, a good-sized gasoline-powered auxiliary electrical generator and an access corridor to the cellar of the house.

"The deceased owners of the place had laid in enough high-quality foodstuffs to have fed a score of men for six months, the water was electrically pumped from an artesian well and the gasoline to power everything was contained in a buried five-thousand-gallon tank. But the reason I stayed there as long as I did was really the elaborate and very powerful short-wave radio. It's because of the couple of months I used that radio that I know as much as I do about what occurred in the rest of the world, long ago, that and my abilities to speak and comprehend a large number of the languages then used.

"In the beginning, I was able to pick up and converse with a very large number of broadcasts—some of them public, commercial- or government-owned, more privately owned and operated—from them, I learned that old hatreds had flared up into new wars, invasions and rebellions nearly everywhere, with all of the deadly side effects of war—wounds, diseases, starvation, terror. I monitored the prideful, often threatening transmissions of winners and the despairing pleas of losers, I conversed with those who would receive my own transmissions. But then the Great Dyings commenced full-force and worldwide.

"Within the short space of three or four weeks, Wahrn, the numbers of transmitters shrank from thousands to hundreds to scores to dozens. They went on going off the air, a few of them doing so quite abruptly, in the very act of transmitting to me or to others. Near the end of my sojourn in that place, there were no more than a dozen other radios still transmitting and receiving in all of the world, death and chaos and war having silenced all the rest forever."

"Why did you leave that place?" beamed Wahrn curiously.

"Part of it was sheer loneliness," Milo replied. "Funny, but when still large portions of the world were swarming with people in the billions, my pleasure was to get completely away from the more built-up, more settled areas for a month or two at the time, never missing human companionship at all. But with mankind rapidly declining to the status of an endangered species all over the world, I began to pine for friendly people among whom I could live, with whom I could talk, eat, drink, share the fast-disappearing human experience."

Mehrdok nodded, beaming, "Yes, I can understand that feeling, Milo. I was a fur trapper, far up to the north and east of here, for three years after I stopped riding as a sword for the traders. That very loneliness is the reason I packed it in and came back here.

"You said that the place was hidden in a canyon. But you had no visitors at all, in all that time?"

Milo grimaced. "No friendly ones, Wahrn. I had had to kill both of the guard dogs in order to get into the house at all—poor beasts, they were only doing the job to which they had been trained. With them dead, I had no warning of intruders until they penetrated to fairly close proximity of the house. But that house had been built with an eye toward defense of it and was more than adequately supplied with firearms, ammunition for them and even items of antipersonnel explosives.

"As you know from my memories, I had been a soldier for a large proportion of my life up until then and I was therefore well versed in techniques of warfare, as I suspected my dead host had been. I used certain of the available materials, in conjuncture with

certain others I manufactured—more silent but no less
deadly than explosives—to render the only two routes
to my hideaway extremely hazardous to any unknow-
ing of just what was just where. The resultant ex-
plosions or screams were my early-warning system.
With that system fully operational, very few spoilers
ever got as far up the canyon as the house.

"The blasted and burned-out hulks blocking the
only real road up the canyon, the charred bodies still
within them, these gave firm notice that the road was
mined and there were more than a few hideous,
frightful surprises awaiting any who tried to come
through the woods and brush on foot or on two-
wheeled vehicles, too. After each attempted foray, I'd
go up and clean and reset the traps, kill any wounded I
happened across, then go back to the radio and the
pure horror it was receiving.

"I like to feel that I served my dead host well, that I
conducted the defense of his property just as he and his
family would have done had they remained alive to do
it. And when I finally did leave that house, I cleaned
it, shut down all of the systems, locked the doors,
bolted the shutters and left all of the mines and booby
traps armed and ready to repel intruders.

"Into the smallest of the vehicles, I packed arms,
ammunition, food, water, extra fuel, bedding and
clothing, along with tools and spare parts for the
vehicle and the firearms. I thought myself to be well
prepared for any eventuality, but—more fool I—it's
wise that I had brought along a backpack, for long
before I reached proximity to any living human
beings, I struck a deep, water-filled crater in the road
surface and wrecked the vehicle far beyond my
abilities of any repair. Knowing of old my capacities at
load-carrying, I filled the backpack with food, some
items of clothing, a pair of boots, most of the gear I'd
used to live off the land up in the mountains, plus

ammunition and magazines and parts for the weapons I was taking with me. I lashed my sleeping bag and a rolled poncho atop the pack, filled two canteens and snapped them to my weapons belt, slung a rifle and headed northwest, in search of my own kind . . . or, rather, what I then assumed were my own kind; in the long years since, I am become less certain.

"Warily, I mostly kept out of sight of the road, moving cross-country and making wide swings to avoid approaching occupied areas by daylight, preferring to reconnoiter under cover of darkness. It was well that I did so, for I witnessed just what happened to two men who simply walked innocently into small towns and subdevelopments. Those residents who had not been driven at least a little mad by the continuing deaths of all their friends and relatives had been given more than sufficient reason by the spoilers to be murderously wary and suspicious of the motives of any strangers, and their tendencies were to shoot first and ask questions later. Under the severe circumstances, no one—and I least of all—could have blamed them for an excess of caution.

"I was shot twice, from a distance, by persons I never even saw, before I decided that until things calmed down somewhat I would be a great deal safer up in the mountains, with the snakes and the bears, then I would in the stinking charnel house that Southern California was by then become. So I sought out and finally found a two-wheel vehicle which had been designed and built for rugged, off-road work, then I headed back west, into the high country, having had my fill of dying but still deadly mankind for a while."

The trail bike took Milo fairly far up into the wild mountains before it sputtered to a stop, out of gasoline. At that point, he reshouldered pack, sleeping bag, poncho, weapons and all and began to hike

farther up while there still was a bit of daylight
remaining to guide him. But he had not gone far when
he cut the track, a relatively fresh track, of a party of
men, perhaps as many as thirty of them, all shod in
Army-issue boots. Keeping to concealment, Milo
paralleled the track until it was become too dark to see
it easily.

Making no unavoidable noises, he made himself a
cold camp, in the heavy brush where he had halted,
denying himself even the small luxury of a pipe, this
night. But he did force himself to sleep for a couple of
hours, after making certain that his L.E.S. 9mm auto
was where he could reach it quickly and easily, once
more silently thanking his dead former host for his
impeccable taste in firearms.

There was no moon when he awakened, but he had
expected none, what with the heavy cloud cover that
had blanketed the sky for the latter half of the day just
past. He made no move to check his wristwatch—
that would have required a brief light which, even if it
did not betray his presence and position, would
destroy his ability to make his way in the darkness for
some time. He stripped himself of every nonessential,
along with anything that might impede his progress
through heavy brush, make a noise at an inopportune
time or reflect light. As weapons on this patrol, he
retained only the Colt M1911A1 automatic pistol—it
did not hold the eighteen 9mm rounds of the L.E.S.,
but he knew damned well that any man he hit with
one of the fat .45 caliber rounds would go down, and
that that was not only always the case with the lighter
9mm—a couple of spare magazines for it, a big Ran-
dall fighting knife and a small, double-edged Russell
boot-knife. Everything else he laid beside the pack,
arranged the camouflaged sleeping bag over all, then
tossed brush and leaves over that. Using the edges of

his bootsoles, he scuffed down to the dirt, urinated there, then smeared the resultant mud onto his forehead, cheekbone lines, chin and the bridge of his nose. That all done, he kicked the leaves back over the wet spot. He now was ready to seek out the men he had been trailing, for better or for worse.

After he had completely scouted out the "encampment" he realized why he had seen no fires, smelled no smoke. Exhaustion, rather than caution, ruled among the emaciated, ill-armed men in their filthy, stained, tattered remnants of uniforms. Many of the sleepers were wearing dirty, blood-splotched bandages, all were many days unshaven and more than a few of the weapons he took from proximity to their sometime bearers were empty of even a single round of ammunition.

When all of the strangers' weapons were safely hidden, Milo went back to his own campsite at the trot and returned laden with all his effects. He had always had a weakness for stray dogs and abandoned cats. Seated, with his back against the thick hole of an ancient tree, he awaited the dawn, his rifle on his lap.

The first man to wake up wore the dark stripes of a master sergeant on the frayed sleeves of his camo battledress. He yawned prodigiously, stretched stiffly, took out a pair of glasses and meticulously polished them before putting them on . . . then he spotted Milo. With a strangled yelp, he reached for a rifle that was no longer where he had put it, then slapped hand to a pistol holster that proved empty. Staring at Milo, who had not raised his rifle or, indeed, moved at all, the noncom reached out and shook the shoulder of the man nearest to him, a man whose single remaining shoulder loop bore the muted embroidery of a lieutenant colonel's silver oak leaf.

"Colonel, *colonel!*" he whispered, imperatively.

"Colonel Crippen, sir, we got comp'ny come to call."

Milo willingly shared out all of his supplies of canned and freeze-dried foodstuffs, found a tiny, icy-cold spring and personally refilled the baker's dozen of sound canteens left among the eighteen enlisted men and five officers, all that now remained of an under-strength battalion of California State Military Reserves.

Colonel Crippen was a bit under average height, but chunky, solid and powerful-looking; Milo guessed the officer's age to be somewhere between fifty and sixty. Considering the circumstances, the quality of his onetime command and the impossible-to-effect orders with which he and his had been sent off, what had happened to him could have easily been predicted, but it still saddened Milo to hear it recounted.

By orders of the state adjutant general—who should have known better, thought Milo—Crippen and his battalion (four hundred and twelve enlisted men, three warrants and twenty-three commissioned officers, equipped with some bare score of Korean War-vintage two-and-a-half-ton trucks, a dozen three-quarter-ton trucks and about that many jeeps that were all about as venerable, a couple of old, boxy field ambulances, and a handful of much newer civilian vehicles pressed into service in the emergency conditions) were sent from the environs of Sacramento via Route 99 toward Bakersfield, where they were supposed to join with a scratch force of National Guardsmen, United States Reservists and a leavening of Regular Air Force from Edwards Air Force Base to try to restore some semblance of order to the areas abutting Los Angeles and San Diego, both of which localities had taken one or more nuclear missile strikes.

The battalion had made it down to Bakersfield in good order, having had only five trucks break down so thoroughly that they had had to be abandoned, stripped and left behind. With a convoy of armed men at his command and a pocketful of state-backed chits countersigned by the governor, Colonel Crippen had experienced scant difficulty in feeding his men or fueling and/or getting emergency repairs on the transport vehicles.

But at Bakersfield, there were no National Guardsmen, not one Reservist and only a few Air Force men, which last group waited in Bakersfield for a couple of days, then headed back to Edwards AFB. The telephones were not working and neither, he discovered, was the radio Colonel Crippen had been issued, nor had anyone bothered to give him spare parts for the thing. When he finally tracked down a civilian repair shop that would even look at the antique marvel, the owner laughed and remarked that he had not seen its like since his days in Vietnam, but he did allow Crippen the use of his own shortwave equipment . . . with the sole proviso that one of the colonel's men would use the bicycle generator to recharge the storage batteries after each use.

At length, Crippen got Sacramento on the radio and finally dropped enough important names to persuade the communications-type to fetch to his set one of the adjutant general's aides, who proved to be no help at all.

"Everyone out there seems to have trouble of one kind or another, Colonel Crippen. I have no idea where the other two units that were supposed to meet you are, but you have received your orders. Just see to it that they are carried out. I suggest, if you need resupply of vehicles and radio equipment, that you route your convoy out to the air base and see if they won't help."

But they would not allow Crippen or any one of his

men any closer than a strongpoint hastily erected around the main gate. A hard-eyed captain sounded honestly sorry.

"Colonel, if it was up to me, I'd let you all in, but it's not. When we first spotted you-all, I rung up my superior and he rung up his and so on and the answer came back, loud and clear: Nobody except Regular Air Force personnel and dependents goes any farther than you are now, on account of it's some real bad diseases killing off the civilians all around here right and left, and the general, he don't want none of whatever it is spreading to this command. Some nervous nellies are already saying that it could be some kind of bacterial warfare stuff.

"Was I you, I'd take my column back north. It don't seem to be as bad, from what we've picked up on the radios, up north as it is here and points south and west of here. We can give you-all water and gas and a couple of days' worth of field rations, but that's all. You-all try to come through onto Edwards anyway, and . . ." He waved a hand at the bristling fortifications behind him. "I'll just have to follow my own orders and do my level best to kill ever mother's son of you. Please don't make me have to do that, colonel."

Major Muldoon, Crippen's executive officer, suggested attacking, forcing their way onto the military reservation, but the colonel would not even consider such a piece of stupidity, saying, "Pat, I think you've got shit for brains. Look, take a good hard look at what those flyboys have got there—heavy machine guns, rockets and God alone knows what else that we can't see, probably, mortars and artillery and a whole hell of a lot more men. And what have we got to throw against them? Rifles, a few automatics and six medium machine guns, not even a single grenade, hand or rifle. There's no earthly way we could sneak up on them, either; they've burned off all of the brush and bulldozed down everything that might give an attacker cover or concealment within rifle range.

"No, we're going to accept what little they're willing to give us, say 'thank you, sir' nicely and then go our way and do what we can for as long as we can with what we have to do it with. Our only other option is to disobey orders and run back to Sacramento with our tails between our legs, and I, for one, have never been good at running away from a fight."

"Well, you're making us run away from this one, David," grumbled Muldoon sourly.

"This would be no fight here, this would be quick, bloody suicide, and if you can't see that plain fact, Pat, maybe I need a clearer-headed exec. Our orders are to help the civil authorities in keeping order; they say not one damned thing about taking on the U.S. Air Force, for whatever reason," snapped Crippen, rapidly losing patience. And when Muldoon opened his mouth to speak again, the colonel cut him off brusquely, saying, "End of discussion, Major Muldoon. I think those trucks up the road, on the base, there, are probably the gas and water and rations the captain mentioned. Captain Peele's the S-4—have him handle the off-loading and reloading. I'm going back up there and see if I can con some ammo and grenades out of that flyboy. We may very well need them . . . soon."

The captain went as far as the constraints of his superiors and the pressing needs of his own base would let him . . . and that was not far: five thousand-round cases of 5.56mm (just about enough to issue eleven more rounds to each man rifle-armed), eight five-hundred-round boxes of 7.62mm ammo to be divided among six machine guns, one hundred fragmentation hand grenades and twenty-five CN gas grenades, plus twenty-five hundred rounds of 9mm ball and less than half that much of .45 ACP ball. Colonel Crippen thanked the man sincerely for everything, for all that he realized that if push really should come to shove where he was going, such piddling amounts would probably only prolong the survival of his unit for bare minutes.

Beyond Four Corners, which had been incorporated into Edwards AFB, the only signs of life along Route 58 were small animals, snakes and the occasional abandoned car or truck. At Barstow, they found out what had happened to the Reservists who had been originally scheduled to meet them at Bakersfield. The men were helping civilians to man the network of entrenchments and hastily erected bunker strongpoints completely surrounding most of the town.

The senior officer of the Reservists, a slender, feisty brigadier general with short-cropped snow-white hair, was curtly apologetic for his heterogeneous unit's failure to rendezvous as planned.

"The NGs met us at San Bernardino, Colonel Crippen, some of the units, both mine and theirs, having had to fight their way there through mobs trying to get their weapons. San Bernardino, when we finally got there, was a plump chicken just waiting to be plucked, most of the law-enforcement types having either been killed or seriously hurt or gone to ground in quite justifiable fear for themselves and their immediate families.

"After a conference of the combined staffs, I decided to leave the NGs down there to harden up the area, establish a perimeter and guard it. Not a few of their people had failed to show up for the muster and so they were radically understrength, and their transport and arms were but little better than are yours. I brought my own force on toward Bakersfield, although on the advice of refugees, I kept off the freeways and made it up 15 and 247 almost without incident until we got to the outskirts of Barstow here.

"The surviving citizens had been forced into the center of town and were there fighting a losing battle against a horde of looters, lunatic refugees, assorted scum and a pack of well-armed outlaw bikers. Well, I sustained a few completely unnecessary casualties trying to do it according to the book on putting down civil disturbances—I even got nicked myself in that fracas.

"That was when one of my subcommanders took over, a Marine Corps Reserve colonel, Mac Rayford. He and his jarheads went through those buggers like shit through a goose. They killed all of the bikers and one hell of a lot of the others and they took no prisoners, wounded or otherwise, on his orders. I think it safe to say that the few who got away from him and his gyrenes are still running and will until they drop, then they'll likely crawl.

"But the sad part of it is, no sooner was the town secured than poor old Mac dropped dead of a heart attack. However, he'd shown all the rest of us, especially me, the proper way, the only way that this business can be fought—no kid gloves, only iron fists. Extend no quarter, shoot first, if you intend to live, forget about the civil rights of your enemies and consider everyone an enemy who cannot immediately prove himself a friend.

"I am indeed sorry that I did not have you contacted to let you know that neither I nor the NGs were going to meet you, but I just never thought to radio you, not with all that was going on here in making this place defensible."

Crippen barked a short, unhumorous laugh. "Even if you had, you couldn't've raised us, general. That radio they issued us up in the capital is a piece of pure antique shit, for which they don't even make parts anymore. But you should've let Sacramento know, at least.

"All that aside, sir, my orders read, in part, to subordinate myself and my command to you at our rendezvous." He saluted and added, "I do so, now, General Brunelle. What are your orders, sir?"

After squinting at the westering sun, General James Brunelle sighed and shook his head. "Do your men have rations? Good. Have the column drive on into town. They'll be directed to a place they can bivouac for the night, take turns showering and eat. You stay with me, colonel—we need to talk about a lot of things."

"The upshot of it, Colonel Moray," said ragged, dirty Crippen as he devoured with his hungry eyes the rabbit slowly browning on its green-wood spit over a bed of hardwood coals, "was that General Brunelle had more than enough men, already, to defend his perimeter. He and the people he had elected to defend were, however, running low on food and fuel; so low were they, in fact, that he already had cleared it with the commander at Twenty-nine Palms to take in his contingent of Marine Corps Reservists, proven-effective combat troops. So, you see, me and mine, we were the very last thing he needed to try and absorb.

"He did give us a few newer, better trucks and jeeps, but we had to siphon the gas for them out of the old ones; he refused to spare us a single drop of his, though he gave us all the lubricants and water we could carry. He gave us spare tires and some tools, too, but no weapons and no ammo, either, not until I agreed to trade him two of my medium machine guns and the CN grenades we'd gotten from the Air Force. Even then, all we got was a few more light automatics, 9mm submachine guns and a few very old .45 grease guns, M3A1s with a single magazine for each one.

"Before he sent us on our way the next morning, he suggested that I find myself an endangered town somewhere and fortify it, then just hunker down until things got back to normal. He also advised me to stay well clear of the Los Angeles and San Diego central areas, for no one knew just what they had been hit with and they could well be virtually glowing with radioactivity.

"For all of the fact that his mechanics and driver, mine and some civilians had worked through the entire night, we were there on those automotive nightmares we had been equipped with in Sacramento, my column lost one truck after another as we drove along on 40 West. All else having failed, with only enough rations for one or maybe two more days, if we stretched it, and not enough ammo for any serious kind of a fight, nor enough gas to keep us all mounted for much longer, I'd just about decided to see if the Twenty-nine Palms Marine Base would take us all in for a while. My thinking was that they had a damned big base with a long perimeter and so might be in need of more bodies to keep it secure.

"We needn't, it developed, have bothered. Like back at Edwards, they wanted only their own kind, Regular or Reserve, but in any case, Marines only, please. Moreover, they not only would not give us any supplies or gas or ammo, they took from us—at the points of heavy weapons!—our last four medium machine guns, the ammo for them and even the jeeps they were mounted on, saying that it was better for them to be in their hands than in the hands of whoever got around to killing us for them. They took most of our grenades, too, noting in passing that they were far too dangerous to be allowed to remain in the hands of state reserves, war-gamers or Boy Scouts. Then they escorted us back to 40 and advised us to go to hell, if we wished, but to stay away from Twenty-nine Palms.

"It was a little later that we lucked onto a gas plaza that had been neither drained dry nor torched. Not only were we able to fill all of the remaining vehicles

and the jerry cans, we found that the place boasted a
five-bay shop, an outdoor grease pit, an artesian well,
its own electrical generator, an air compressor and a
whole mess of tools, parts, fluids and what have you.
Even the coffee and soft-drink machines still worked,
and we found some cases of beer, juices, candy bars,
smoked sausages, jerky, chips and salted nuts. So we
just set up camp in and around the place and went to
work on our transport . . . after we'd buried the seven
bodies we found. Five men and a woman and a child,
dead, without a mark on them.

"The next morning, a dozen of my men were down,
violently ill, feverish, unable to hold even water on
their stomachs, racked with cramps and diarrhea. Our
medics tried everything they knew or had in the
ambulances, but nothing worked; every one of those
men were dead before the second morning. More
turned up sick even as we were getting set to bury the
first lot, and included in the new cases were both of
our medics, leaving us only one trained man, our
battalion surgeon, Captain Weeks.

"That loudmouthed fool of an executive officer, Pat
Muldoon, had to remark to me in public that the
twelve men all had had a part in burying the dead
folks we had found when we got there. After that,
those few of us who hadn't panicked had to wrap the
bodies in trash bags and plastic sheeting and, finally,
cut-up truck-top canvas before any of the others would
dump them into graves. Not only that, but it was
damned few of the men who would any longer help
Doc Weeks tend the sick. They were dying, really,
because he couldn't save or help any of them.

"Sometime around dawn of our second morning
there, two hundred and ninety-two men and officers
took the best of the remaining trucks, their weapons,
most of the ammo and almost all of the food and split
out. Muldoon was stricken by then, and it was his
shouts and pleas and screams and curses yelled after

them for leaving him behind that woke the rest of us up. From the bastard's ravings before he died, it seems that he was the prime mover in planning the mutiny and mass desertion. I hope the son of a bitch is roasting in the deepest, foulest pit of hell at this very minute!"

Then the rabbit was done and Colonel David Crippen stopped talking for a while.

Chapter X

Milo and Wahrn turned the skinned, gutted and partially butchered deer carcass over to the women, set about first removing the useful hooves and teeth, cracked open the skull and scooped out the brains for use in tanning the hide, then pegged out the hide itself for fleshing and scraping. Everything done, the two men strolled down to the shallows at the edge of the shrinking lake to lave their bodies of the blood and sweat and squashed insects.

As they washed themselves, standing waist-deep in the sun-warmed water, ignoring the brushings and nippings of fingerling fish busy at feeding on the blood and salt sweat on their calves and thighs, Wahrn beamed, "So, please tell me, Milo, what ever happened to this unfortunate officer, this Colonel Crippen? Did he and his men all die of the strange disease, too?"

Milo shook his dripping head. "Not during the weeks I stayed with them, Wahrn . . . though what happened to him and them after that is anybody's guess, of course. They were the epitome of a hard-luck bunch, but I hope they all got back to Sacramento alive and in one piece.

"I kept them near to where I'd found them, though I

did move to a better campsite. Those mountains were aswarm with rabbits that year, so I rigged dozens of rabbit snares, showed them all how to build shelters and bough beds, collected edible wild plants and showed them how to heat rocks in a fire, then use them to simmer a meat-and-plant stew in a green hide. I found a frigid spring-fed stream nearby and badgered them all into washing themselves and their clothing, then did what little I could to aid them in repairing it.

"After a week or so of hot, regular meals, sleep and regular, controlled physical exercise, I marched them slowly, in short stages, south, down to a tiny village I'd swung wide of on my way up into the mountains. The few people still left there were all dead, and animals had been at most of the bodies, so many were by then little more than skeletons, ill concealed by flapping rags. That's how fast the Great Dyings ran their deadly course, Wahrn; only a week or so before, that village had been active, with armed men standing guard over it, yet bare days later, it was a village of only the dead.

"Dave Crippen made some noises about burials, but I pointed out that his men still might be a little wary of such onerous details and that, in any case, Nature was well on the way to recycling the corpses. The colonel was also stubbornly insistent on contacting his superiors in Sacramento, but all of the village telephones proved to be dead and we could find no way of powering such few radio transmitters as we came across.

"However, the village, small as it was, did provide us with a fair amount of food, some firearms— mostly shotguns, hunting rifles and pistols, though with two or three military-type weapons, as well —modest quantities of ammunition, clothing and boots, tools and utensils, as well as enough rugged vehicles to mount us all and gas to fuel them.

"I headed us south and west, back to the house

hidden in the blind canyon. I severely cautioned them all, then led the convoy through my outer defenses, noting as I did so that these defenses had obviously claimed more victims since I had left. But the house, when at last we got to it, proved inviolate; no one had had what it took to get that far in. The blackened, rusting vehicles and the rotted human remnants in my man-traps had vastly impressed the covey of State Military Reserves.

"When we passed one particularly gruesome example of the fate of trespassers on posted land, Crippen gulped and asked, "*You* built all these *things*, Mr. Moray? Where in God's name did you learn to do things this brutal? I've figured out days ago that you were ex-military, but I didn't know that even the Marine Corps would teach such dirty tricks as this to be used in warfare."

"You learn to do what you have to do to keep your own men alive and kill or incapacitate as many as possible of the enemy in any damned way you can, Crippen," Milo replied, adding, "I was never a Marine, though I was a U.S. Army Ranger officer . . . among other things."

When they finally made it out of the brushy woods and into the clearing and the house was visible, Crippen perked up out of his dark brooding and said, "Why, I know this place. I was once at a small conclave of State Military Reserve officers here. I didn't recognize the approach because the other time I came in by chopper, from up north. This is General Jerry Noonan's place. You say everybody was dead when you first got here, Mr. Moray?"

"Jerry Noonan?" asked Milo. "Isn't he that retired type who has been asshole-deep in politics these last few years? I've read about him, I think. But where the hell would a retired Army officer get the kind of loot it must have taken to build and outfit a place like this?"

"From his wife, Mr. Moray—his second wife was one of the heiresses to the Stiles fortune. But I don't think that money was the only reason he married her, despite rumors to the contrary; yes, she was a bit older than he was, but they seemed quite happy and devoted to each other nonetheless."

Milo tried hard to repress a shudder as an icy chill ran down the full length of his spine. Which one? Which of the little girls he had adopted, fathered, raised as his own, was that aging woman he had buried here?

Exercising iron self-control, he asked, "You met her, then, Colonel Crippen? Do you recall her Christian name?"

Crippen wrinkled his brows, then responded, "Why . . . I believe it was some French name . . . ahh, Gabrielle, I think. Yes, that was it, Gabrielle Stiles Noonan. Why?"

"Oh, no particular reason, just curiosity," said Milo, but thinking of little Gaby as she had been when first he saw her, riding in a dog cart at the farm in Loudon County, Virginia, more than fifty years ago. And he remembered her as a gangly thirteen-year-old with an achingly beautiful face, competently handling the reins of the big Thoroughbred she sat so easily, greeting him when he returned from the Korean War.

Her voice still had its little-girl quality, but her words had been those of an adult woman, spoken in the pure, accentless French of her mother. "You, monsieur, are a pure and unadulterated man, and if Mama still did not live, I would make you mine, immediately. Please promise me that when the time comes for me to marry, you will find for me a brave, gentle and tender officer just like you. I so wish that you really were my father by blood, monsieur, for a son like you would be my dearest pride and treasure."

Gaby's first husband, a young USMA graduate, had

died in Milo's arms, early on in the country's involvement in the Vietnam quagmire. That was when she and her brother had gotten involved in the leftist-controlled antiwar movement. Gaby, thankfully, had possessed intelligence, maturity and strength of will to get out of the thing before it irrevocably warped her mind as it did so many others. Her brother, on the other hand—and despite Milo's attempt to drag him out of it, away from bad companions—had sunk into violently radical Marxism and perversion and had finally taken to the drugs that ended his life so prematurely.

When the Army had brought Milo back from Southeast Asia in the early 1970s and hurriedly retired him because, according to the Department of Defense records, he was far too old a man to remain on the active list, he had gotten involved with various foreign governments that proved more than willing to hire the services of an officer with such impressive credentials, regardless of his official age. Spending, as he had been, more and more time out of the United States and never knowing just what fate the future might hold for a man in such perilous places and situations, he had deposited a largish chunk of fluid assets in a Swiss bank account for personal use and possible emergencies, then instructed the law firm which had handled his and the estate affairs since the mid-1940s to draw up a new document dividing the Stiles fortune and properties among his three living adoptive children—Gaby, Melusine, twin of by then dead Michel, and Per, by then in hospital getting used to a replacement for the leg a landmine had taken.

Once he had signed the documents, made the transfers official, he had taken advantage of certain aspects of his new employment to drop out of sight of all who had known him in his earlier life, even "his" children. He found it quite a relief to thus change identities, for all that the people among whom he now moved never, ever asked questions the answers to which might be embarrassing, lest someone so question the interrogator; not that Milo could have given an intelligent answer to many of the inconsistencies, anyway. He, least of all, understood just why, at an estimated minimum seventy years of age, he looked no whit different from the Milo Moray who had enlisted in the United States Army years before the Second World War.

In the company of his family and those who had known him for long periods of time, his unchanged, unchanging physical appearance had been an embarrassment, to say the least. Here, in this new life, his peers simply assumed that he had had skilled plastic surgery at the same time he had changed his name and obtained new, forged passports and documents, for not a few of them had done one or more of these very things at some time or some place in their checkered pasts.

For some years, until the venerable attorney died of old age and a bad heart, Milo had been able to keep track of the three kids and their ups and downs of life through John Bannister. Per had taught at West Point, briefly, gone out to Montana to personally check on some family holdings there and ended up marrying and settling down in that state; he had taught himself to ride horses again, sired several children and eventually, trading shrewdly on his war record and fortune, entered quite successfully into first state, then national politics.

Poor little Melusine had had a rougher time of it. Her judgment with regard to people had proved almost as faulty as had been that of her deceased twin and had resulted in a succession of unhappy, mercifully short marriages to handsome but shallow men who had all developed to be far more interested in her wealth, the status and material objects it could buy, than in her. Finally, disillusioned and teetering on the verge of insanity, sodden with alcohol and addicted to various drugs, the miserable woman had left a hospital to live in the adjacent convent of the nursing order. After some years, she took holy orders and signed her third of the patrimony over to the church. Bannister had assured Milo that her letters and the single, brief meeting he had had with her had convinced him that Melusine Moray had at last found happiness and true contentment. At the turn of events, Milo had not been able but to wonder just what her true father's opinion would have been; though deeply religious in his own way, General Jethro Stiles' opinions of organized religions in general had been unprintable in any known language.

Gaby had remarried at about the time Milo had been forcibly repatriated and pensioned off. He had taken part in the wedding ceremony, had again given her away to a young paraplegic a couple of years her senior, a man who had been a classmate of her late husband's and who had, like him, been one of Milo's junior officers in Vietnam. Thanks to modern medical advances, Gaby had had two children by her second husband before he died by his own hand in one of his periodic fits of despondency, whereupon she had settled down to making a full-time job of raising her children.

But after old Bannister had died, Milo had gradually lost any really personal contact with the survivors of his onetime family, which explained why he had not even known of his Gaby's marriage to the vital, charismatic former-general, Noonan, who had among other things been frequently mentioned as a prime contender for the then-in-power party's next presidential campaign, which now, of course, would never take place.

In the huge, sprawling home that had been Noonan's, even Crippen and his men were not unduly crowded, and although all of the frozen and refrigerated foods were long since spoiled and had to be buried, there still were enough supplies of canned and otherwise preserved foods to keep them adequately, with venison and other game brought in by Milo, Master Sergeant Lyon and two or three other experienced hunters.

After three days of hourly broadcasts, they finally got a response from the state capital at Sacramento. Crippen had had to go to great lengths and into meticulous and personal detail before he was able to achieve belief as to his identity. Since no one had seen him and his force or radioed of his whereabouts since his column had left Barstow, he and all of them had been assumed dead either of the plagues or of hostile action.

Once they were certain that it really was Colonel Crippen, however, the governor himself began to transmit, sounding very tired and more than a little distraught. "David? It's truly you, then? How many men are with you? That few, huh? Well, even that many is better than none at all, I suppose. How far from here are you? *At Noonan's place?* How the hell did you . . . never mind. Have you got transport? Good, get up here just as fast as you can with all the arms you can scrape up and plenty of ammo. We're in terrible need of more disciplined troops; half the city is dead or dying and the other half is starving and on the verge of riot and rebellion. . . . No, I won't order you, David. I know that you and those with you must have gone through pure hell already. But I plead with you, rather. You're needed desperately, colonel . . . no, I guess it's general, now, since you're the highest-ranking State Military Reserve officer left alive."

Two days later, while helping to make certain that

all of the vehicles were in tip-top condition, Milo accidentally found General Noonan's hidden armory of what had, until recently, been completely illegal weapons and equipment. Strong and strictly enforced federal and state and local laws had forbidden the ownership by private citizens of such things as hand-held surface-to-air missiles, anti-armor rockets, light mortars, grenade launchers and automatic firearms, not to mention grenades, other military explosives and chemical-warfare agents. Stacked along one side of the rock-walled room was enough small-arms ammunition to start a small war.

When at last they all departed, in vehicles now altered to provide somewhat less comfort but much more protection, they were become far more formidable a force than anything just then moving through the all but deserted landscape of the once-populous State of California. Such few individuals and small groups as they saw along Route 40 took but a single look at the bristling rifles and automatics and afforded the column a wide—a very wide—berth.

At one point, where three semis parked athwart the road served as a roadblock, a single rocket blasting the centermost trailer apart served as a more than sufficient reason for the scruffy types manning the point to recall urgent business . . . *elsewhere.* After the last of Crippen's vehicles had cleared the obstruction, Milo drove the three tractors into roadside ditches and set them all afire. The three-wheeled trail bike that he found there he put to immediate and personal use.

They smelled Barstow long before they got within sight of the place. There were corpses everywhere anyone looked, and the shots they fired off in the hopes of bringing anyone still living out onto the streets only served to send overfed buzzards scurrying and flapping about over their grisly interrupted repasts. There were flies everywhere, thick, metallic-sheened swarms of them, and the rotting, rat-gnawed bodies still on the perimeter defenses housed clumps of fat, writhing, wriggling maggots, shiny white or yellow.

The Crippen column wasted no more time, only seeking out enough gas to top off their tanks, retrieving a few weapons and some ammunition, then heading west on Route 58 toward Bakersfield and points north.

Milo determined that Edwards Air Force Base must still be at least partially manned. He never saw anyone or got any answer to his shouts, but he was fired on from at least three points of the fortified main gate. Crippen readily agreed to bypass Edwards.

Bakersfield, when they got there, was Barstow on a far larger scale, sans a perimeter worthy of the name, but including signs of fires, combats and large-scale lootings. It, like Barstow, stank too badly to contemplate staying any longer than absolutely necessary, so they fueled and left the town and its current occupants to Nature's undertakers.

That night, in their well-guarded camp at what had been a rest area, Milo announced his intention to Crippen. "You'll make it now, general, if anybody can and if you pay attention to Sergeant Weeks. I'll be leaving you in the morning, west, into the mountains, taking only what I originally had, plus that trail bike, some spare gas and water and two or three days' worth of food."

Crippen snorted. "You're loco, Moray, you know that? Just how long do you think you'll last alone? Who'll care for you if you get hurt or sick?

"Besides, a man like you would be invaluable up in Sacramento now. I'll probably make a lousy, piss-poor general officer, but you, now, you'd make a fine one."

"No, thank you, Crippen," replied Milo. "I've been

a general, and it's not all it's cracked up to be, you'll find, just much more work and a crushing load of responsibilities and . . ."

Just then, Master Sergeant Weeks dropped his coffee cup and, wide-eyed, exclaimed, "*Now* I recollect you, sir! Gen'rul, thishere is nobody else but the man the ARVNs called *le saint diabolique.* Back when he was a very unofficial U.S. Army observer with the French, he escaped someway from Dien Bien Phu, th'ough the whole fucking Vietminh army and ever'thin'. He come back as a U.S. army adviser and then stayed there for over ten years, off and on, a whole helluva lot of it up in them damn mountains with the Montagnards, and they purely worshiped him, too, they claimed he was a god come down to earth in the shape of a man, that he could grow back any part he lost like a fence lizard grows back a tail and that couldn' nuthin kill him. I *know*, gen'rul! I never did see him 'cept at a distance, but I talked to 'Nards and ARVNs as had done knowed him."

Turning to Milo, the sergeant demanded with respect, "Why don't you look your age, sir? You're a whole lot older'n I am."

Milo had not fielded such a question in a long time, but he still remembered how. "I have always prided myself in keeping fit, sergeant. And did you ever hear of plastic surgery?"

They talked on into the dark night, but Crippen, knowing within himself that he would not be able to change Milo's mind, made weaker and increasingly weaker attempts to dissuade his savior's departure, then ceased entirely. The last couple of hours before all retired for what was left of the night were filled with Milo's reminiscences and anecdotes from his years as a mercenary officer in Africa, the Middle East and various parts of Central and South America.

When the Crippen column headed north, Milo revisited the Bakersfield area long enough to loot a couple of good bows, arrows and accessories and some odds and ends of general camping equipment, then made his way up into the mountains again, seeking to breathe air clean of the cloying stench of decomposing humanity.

Something over a month later, he came down, found a jeeplike vehicle and drove directly to the Noonan place with its generator and powerful short-wave radio. After cleaning the main refrigerator-freezer, he stalked and shot a fat, sizable doe, gathered wild fruits and vegetables from the woods and settled down for a while with the radio.

But it was days before he raised an answering set. Sacramento was unresponsive, by day or by night, and he tried both, at different times each day. It was at night, nearly midnight, that he at last got an answer, such as it was.

"Where are you located, unidentified station? Are you private, governmental or commercial, or are you military?"

"You want to know one hell of a lot without divulging anything yourself," Milo replied bluntly. "But in answer, I'm a private station a bit northeast of what used to be San Diego, California. Now, who are you and where are you?"

"I am . . . we are, rather, we were a scientific research facility, located in . . . Florida, and that's all you need to know. Have you been able to raise Washington, D.C.?"

Milo answered. "I haven't tried . . . at least, not recently. It was nuked, you know, one of the first urban areas hit, and hit by more than just one missile, I've been told. If you're some kind of hush-hush government outfit, how come *you* didn't know that?"

"What we are or were and our sponsorship and funding is none of your concern," was the somewhat haughty reply. "Who, exactly, are you? How many of you are there?"

"There's just me, buster. I'm a retired Army officer, speaking to you from the home of the late General Jerry Noonan. Now tell me a bit more about you. What part of Florida are you in? Did as many die off there as did here?" asked Milo, not really expecting a straight answer from the fanatically security-conscious type on the other radio.

"The Cent . . . ahh, we are in north-central Florida," said the disembodied voice, somewhat hesitantly. "How many died out there?"

"What I've seen of California is wall-to-wall corpses, old and young, male and female, of every race and color," Milo stated baldly. "I'd guesstimate that at least, *at least* ninety percent of the former population of this state is dead of disease, starvation, violence or just plain fear. What percentage died back east, there?"

After a longish pause, the voice said stiffly, "That is classified information."

Exasperatedly, Milo snapped, "Buster, you take your fucking stupid, now-needless and silly security shit and shove it way up your arse. Hear me? Either that or jam it up whoever has been prompting you there. There's not all that much gasoline left for the generator powering this radio, and I'll be fucked if I'm going to waste airtime on a turd-brained fuck-face and his peckerhead stooge. End of transmission!"

His second contact, later that same night, was an anomaly and a one-in-a-million chance both rolled into one. He received and replied to a South African military field-radio transmission and found himself, to his surprise and pleasure, talking to an old friend from his own days in Africa, an officer named Melleneaux.

"Jan, is that you? How the hell are you, you old reprobate? I'd've thought they'd've hung or shot you, by now."

"And just who the bloody hell are you, Yank? Get to hell off this band immediately, or I'll have *you* shot. This is a military transmission, an *urgent* military transmission. Hear me?"

"I don't think you can shoot that far, Jan. I'm near the western coast of North America. This is Milo, Milo Moray, Jan." Milo chuckled into the microphone.

"Milo? It's really you, Milo? Damn, it's good to hear your voice again, though I'd much rather see you—we could certainly use you, just now. The kaffirs are dying like so many flies, both the good ones and the bad, the coloreds and a good many of the Asians, too. But this far, damn-all of us. I've just accepted the unconditional surrender of the Cuban forces for all of Angola—they were damned near all that were left alive in the whole bloody country. Their senior commander, one Jaime Villalobos something-or-other, seems bloody well anxious to sign his lot up with us, and Pretoria will likely accept him and them. If we stay well and the damned pitiful kaffirs keep dying, we'll end owning most of the damned continent we . . ."

Then, heartbreakingly, the voice dissolved into static and Milo never again was able to raise response from that wavelength, try as he might and did.

The next morning, he monitored a governmental broadcast from São Paulo, Brazil. The entirety of the broadcast, done in both the Brazilian dialect of Portuguese and in New World Spanish, was a grim warning that Brazil definitely possessed nuclear capability, owned appropriate means of delivery and would not hesitate to nuke the population centers and military installations of anyone who violated Brazilian borders "during the current state of emergency." Milo could raise no reply to any of his attempts to transmit to São Paulo. However, during the course of one such attempt, he picked up an answer from a totally unexpected quarter.

Vasili Vlasov identified himself as captain of a factory ship which also was flagship of a present mini-armada of his ship and three trawlers, proceeding from the South Pacific to Vladivostok. His command of English was marginal, at best, but Milo spoke excellent Russian, fortunately.

He had tried to put in at a Chilean port and been fired upon; one of his original four trawlers had been hit and sunk there, and another had been damaged by shellfire.

"The bastards accused me and the Motherland of having started this entire insanity, of initiating the nuclear exchanges and of having filled the air of all the world with poisons and deadly germs. Why did the United States of America do this atrocity to Russia and the rest of our world? Can you tell me that?"

Milo sighed. "Captain Vlasov, a couple of months back, I sent transmissions to, received transmissions from and/or monitored transmissions from most parts of the world. The consensus then was that neither your country nor mine started the short, deadly fracas . . . we just finished it and ourselves, and quite possibly all of our species, too."

Vlasov's heavy sigh came over the airwaves. "It's as I suspected, *Tovarich* Moray, just as I suspected all along, then, I suppose. Who do you think did start it?"

"The majority of the people I listened to or talked to, a couple of months or so back, before the really large-scale dyings started, suspected three instigators —Libya, Israel, and India, in just that order of probability."

"Most likely those damned aggressive, land-hungry, warmongering, racist Israelis, then," rumbled Vlasov. "It was many times said that they would not be happy until they owned the entire Middle East and all of North Africa, as well."

"My vote would go against Libya, captain," stated Milo. "The inhabitants of India always hated each other far worse than they hated non-Indians, and teetering on the verge of a three- or four-sided civil war as they were, I doubt seriously that they would've gone outside of India in search of trouble.

"But Libya, now, that's another kettle of fish, captain. Ruled over by an aging, egomaniacal dictator who has alienated every neighbor with which he shares a border and quite a few countries far removed from his borders, as well. He considered himself to be the savior of both Islam and all of Africa, at one time or another. I suspect that he finally lost the last vestige he still owned of sanity and commenced hurling nuclear missiles at every real and imagined enemy and that he kept it up until he ran out of missiles or until Egypt and Israel put paid to his long-overdue accounts."

"Hmmm," muttered Vlasov. "That makes a good bit of sense to me, *tovarich*. Before Vladivostok went off the air, they reported to us that the first nuclear strikes were all in the far southwest of the Motherland, and in parts of Rumania, Yugoslavia, Albania and Bulgaria, even a few in both Greece and Turkey and at least one on Rome, in Italy. It was days later, I have heard, that the big strikes on the Motherland were launched from China and the United States of America. Yes, Libya could very well indeed be the culpable country. But what can now be done to retaliate, to punish such infamy, and who is now left capable of doing anything to them?"

"From what little I heard, in my earlier days on this

radio," said Milo dryly, "Egypt, Israel and France took care of the matter quite thoroughly. Libya's population centers are now mostly flat and probably glow in the dark."

"Good!" snapped Vlasov, forcefully and with clear feeling. Then he said, "*Tovarich* Moray, you have the sound of an honest man, and you must be a very strong man, as well, to have retained your reason in and among the horrors you have described in that place. I will tell you, I will go aboard one of the faster trawlers and we will steam to the Port of San Diego. You can meet us there, come aboard and return with me to Vladivostok. What do you say, *tovarich*?"

"San Diego was nuked, captain, hit by two or three smaller missiles, probably launched from just offshore by submerged submarines."

After a few moments of rustling paper noises, Vlasov asked, "Well, then, we could as easily put in to, let's see . . . Los Angeles or Santa Barbara or San Francisco, if you could easily get that far north in time to meet us. If as few people are now alive in the whole world as you have estimated to me, I think that we few must begin to forget outdated nationalism and band together in true internationalism."

"You're right, of course, Captain Vlasov—Vasili—but your worthy sentiments have come a bit too late for any of us, I'm afraid. Yes, I could get to any of the cities and ports you've mentioned, were I not afraid of going close to them, that is."

"Nuclear destruction? All of them? All of those lovely, lovely cities, *tovarich*?"

"Yes, Vasili, and not just them, either. Portland, Seattle-Tacoma, Vancouver, in Canada, Chicago, Houston, New Orleans, Washington, D.C., New York, Boston, Norfolk, Philadelphia. And that's just on this continent. If you have an alternate home port or even if you don't, steer clear of Vladivistok, my friend. I intercepted a transmission from a Japanese Self-Defense Force frigate that had *seen* that port hit and were so rattled that they didn't even encode their message to their base."

"Frankly, I have long thought that that was what happened, but I have tried hard to delude myself into the thought that it was not that way. It was easier thinking, you see, Tovarich Milo, for my dear wife, some of our children and most of our grandchildren live . . . lived nearby to the port. I suppose that I am alone, completely alone, now. Since it is so, then I just must make my family those brave mariners and fishermen who depend upon me."

"That's the best thing you can do, under the harsh, bitter circumstances, my friend Vasili," Milo assured the suffering man. "It clearly demonstrates to all the great strength of your character, your self-discipline, your dedication to the welfare of your subordinates. You're one hell of a lot like me. If only I could've met you sometime . . ."

"*Tovarich*, I still could bring a trawler for you. Give me the name of a nonradioactive port and I will quickly plot a course and tell you when you must be there." The Russian's invitation bore the undertones of a plea.

"No, Vasili," replied Milo. "No, you—any men like you—are surely needed desperately in your motherland, just now. You must return to help those who have survived everything so far to survive the coming winter. Coming here to fetch me would likely add weeks to your journey home, and those weeks could cost lives, many lives. I could not be happy with those lives on my conscience. Besides, I must soon see what I can do about succoring some of my own people, I suppose."

Milo never again was able to communicate with those Russians or any other, unless the broadcasts he monitored from Erevan, in Soviet Armenia, were counted. All through one twelve-hour period, the same message was broadcast by several people speaking some twenty different European and Asian languages. The message was the same in every language that Milo could understand and probably in those he could not understand, as well: it was the announcement of establishment of a completely free and independent State of Armenia, comprising parts of the Russian Caucasus, eastern Turkey, Iraq, Iran and northern Syria. Even as he listened to the broadcasts, Milo wondered if and how the Armenians would be able to conquer and/or hold so much territory. After that one day, there were no more broadcasts from the environs of Erevan, nor any response to his attempts to reach them.

He stayed on the radio until the underground gasoline tank was dry, then drained the tank of the vehicle in which he had arrived as well, using an absolute minimum of electricity for other things in order to keep the radio on the air. But all things must have an eventual end, and at long last the generator ground to a halt for lack of fuel. Had there been more than just the one storage battery, he might have rigged up a bicycle generator to keep them charged enough for a few air hours each day, but there was only the one left, and it would not have been sufficient for the needs of Noonan's elaborate and powerful and energy-gobbling equipment.

He spent one day tripping or disarming all of the booby traps guarding the approaches to Noonan's place, cleaned the house and secured it against weather or animals, but did not lock the closed doors. The next morning, he shouldered his gear and weapons and set his feet to the steep, narrow trail that led up the back wall of the box canyon, headed once more for the mountains. Such remnants as now remained of mankind could wait for a while.

Epilogue

Milo's mind had been greatly eased when neither Wahrn Mehrdok nor Kahl Renee had been able to identify the pelt of the huge, vicious weaselly beast killed out on the prairie.

"It's like nothing I've seen around these parts, Milo," Mehrdok had stated emphatically, adding, "And a critter that big and toothy would be damned long in the forgetting. Although when I was trapping away up north of here, I did hear a tale of a critter that could've been his kind, said to live somewhere to the west of where I was. Could be that this one strayed down from there, last winter, maybe. I sure hope that was how it was, leastways. Critters like this is the last things we need hereabouts."

Over the weeks, Rehnee and Mehrdok had ridden back to their community a couple of times to assure the people that they were still alive, meant to dwell with the nomads for a bit longer and were in no way prisoners or hostages in need of rescue.

With both threats—the possibility of a raid in force by Dirtmen 'and predation of the horse herd by another of the huge, strange beasts—neutralized, Milo and his people could relax their guard, relax it as much as the naturally wary Horseclansfolk ever did.

Wahrn Mehrdok slipped easily into the nomad life, and even the more provincial Kahl Rehnee showed that he could soon adapt to such a style of living free upon the plains and prairie, with no onerous birth-to-death bonds to one small plot of land. Also, the prairiecat Snowbelly, who—like all prairiecats—was a far better telepath than any human, had discovered in Rehnee a spark of quiescent mindspeak talent or ability and was nurturing it, exercising and developing it.

Spotted One, the jaguar-turned-prairiecat, found and enlarged an animal burrow near to the pasturage of the horse herd and there threw a litter of four blind mewling kittens, each of the beastlets only slightly larger than a grown rat. As she flatly refused to bring or allow twolegs to fetch her litter into camp where they could be completely safe from predatory animals, Milo ordered a sizable part of the butchering debris from each day's hunt deposited at the mouth of the underground den—the offal and lights of herbivores so keenly relished by felines—so that Spotted One could be within sound if not sight of the den as much as possible and be spared long hunts.

Milo, Bard Herbuht and the other nomads were bursting with curiosity to see just what prairiecat-jaguar hybrids looked like, but Spotted One was grimly adamant; she promised death to any—with two legs, four or none at all—who essayed to come near her kittens. Therefore, the best Milo and the other mindspeakers could do was to enter into Spotted One's mind, mesh theirs with it and view the newborn felines through her eyes, which showed them only that the kittens were about of a size with prairiecat kittens of the same age and that they were all four possessed of a constant hunger and of prodigious appetites for fresh mother's milk. With this distinctly unsatisfying satisfaction, the nomads all had to be satisfied.

Then, of a day, Milo, Wahrn Mehrdok, Kahl Rehnee and Snowbelly had ranged far, far out to the west on a hunt, so that the two would-be nomads might learn the relative ease of hunting in company with a prairiecat. They had done well, and three antelope carcasses were tied onto the packhorses as earnest of their efforts. It was Mehrdok who, after tying the last knots, looked up and spoke aloud, in quiet warning.

"Milo, Kahl, look, there to the far west, obscuring the sun. It can be nothing but a prairie fire, a big one from the looks of it, too.

"Kahl, ride back to the farms and tell Daiv Djahnstuhn about this. Tell him to take some men and boys to the west bank of the creek and burn off all the brush for a half a mile beyond it. Set the womenfolks and kids to wetting down roofs, sidings, hayricks, anything that even looks flammable. Drive in and tightly pen up all the stock, too.

"Milo, best thing we can do for you and yours is to try to set backfires around your camp, drive the horses into the lake shallows and try to keep the critters there until the big fire has gone its way. Well, man, time's a-wastin'—are we all to be alive this time tomorrow, let's get going!" A note of urgency and agitation was now borne in the Dirtman's tone.

But Milo continued sitting his horse and smiling. "Wahrn," he said gently, "you're wrong. That's no fire-smoke, yonder; that's dust, the trail dust thrown up by a moving clan and its herds."

He mindspoke Snowbelly, beaming, "Cat brother, try to range a prairiecat mind off there to the southwest."

A split second later, the big cat beamed back, "Not just one cat mind, Uncle Milo, but almost as many as I have claws on my feet. And I know those minds, too, they are of the cat clan septs that ride with Clans

Staiklee and Gahdfree. The twolegs are less than a mile behind the cats."

Milo beamed his thanks to the cat, then turned to the two farmers. "Clans Staiklee and Gahdfree will shortly arrive, gentlemen. Let us get our kills back to camp and begin to prepare a suitable reception for the chiefs and subchiefs."

At a fast amble, the three men, the five horses and the bounding cat headed east across the face of the rolling grasslands.

About the Author

ROBERT ADAMS lives in Seminole County, Florida. Like the characters in his books, he is partial to fencing and fancy swordplay, hunting and riding, good food and drink. At one time Robert could be found slaving over a hot forge making a new sword or busily reconstructing a historically accurate military costume, but, unfortunately, he no longer has time for this as he's far too busy writing.

For more information about Milo Morai, Horseclans, and forthcoming Robert Adams books contact the NATIONAL HORSECLANS SOCIETY, P.O. Box 1770, Apopka, FL 32704-1770.